J. Moyr Smith

**Tales of Old Thulê**

J. Moyr Smith

**Tales of Old Thulê**

ISBN/EAN: 9783337025335

Printed in Europe, USA, Canada, Australia, Japan

Cover: Foto ©Andreas Hilbeck / pixelio.de

More available books at **www.hansebooks.com**

THE SANDALS OF HERMÓD.                    P. 191.

COLLECTED AND ILLUSTRATED BY

# J. MOYR SMITH

Es war ein König in Thule
Gar treu bis an das Grab
Dem sterbend seine Buhle
Einen goldnen Becher gab.—Goethe.

PHILADELPHIA

J. B. LIPPINCOTT & CO.

1879

# CONTENTS.

|  |  | PAGE |
|---|---|---|
| 1. Rashycoat | | 1 |
| 2. Rollo and the Magic Sword | | 26 |
| 3. Jack and the Fairy Princess | | 59 |
| 4. The Brownie in the Pantry | | 75 |
| 5. Prince Coralin | | 89 |
| 6. The Trial of the Suitors | | 110 |
| 7. The Sandals of Hermod | | 120 |
| 8. The Golden Glove | | 194 |

HERE was once a king in Thulé who had the most beautiful woman in the world for his

wife. Whenever she went abroad, all the people
left their work and ran to look at her, for her
face was as lovely, and her shape was as perfect,
as Freyja* herself. They had one daughter,
who was the prettiest little princess that ever
was seen, and they all lived together peacefully
and happily till the princess was twelve years
old. Then the queen fell sick, and though
the king tried everything to cure her, she gradually got worse and worse, and they all knew
that she was dying.

The only thing that troubled the dying
queen's mind was the fear that the king, her
husband, after her death would marry somebody that would be a cruel stepmother to her
daughter. So she made him promise that he
would not marry any woman but one whom the
dying queen's clothes would fit exactly.

The queen died and was buried, and the
king mourned for her for a year or more. Then
he thought he would like to marry again, so
he went through the country trying to get a

* The Norse goddess of beauty.

wife whose shape was like his last queen's. He and his counsellors collected all the finest-shaped and prettiest ladies and took them to the king's house to try on the queen's clothes. But the clothes suited none of them: some were too short, some were too tall, some were too thick, and some were too thin, so they had all to go home again. The king tried and tried to get a new wife, and at the same time keep his promise to his dead queen, but he could not find anybody to fulfil the conditions he had agreed to.

Four years had passed since the queen's death, and still the king had not been able to get a wife. The princess was now sixteen, and had as lovely a face and as fine a shape as her mother. One day she went into her mother's room and saw all her dresses hanging against the wall. She tried on one and then another, and they all fitted her easily At last she tried on the richest and finest, which had been the queen's wedding dress, and it fitted her as neatly as her own skin.

As she was standing looking at herself in

the glass, the king, her father, came in and saw
her.  He started back, thinking how like the
princess was to the queen when he first married
her.  Then the thought came into his wicked and
foolish head, that, as his daughter was the only
one the queen's clothes fitted, he must marry her.

The princess laughed at first, thinking he was
joking; but finding he was resolved to marry
her, she ran out of the house, and sat in the wood
sobbing as if her heart would break.

As she sat sobbing and weeping, a wee old
man with a long grey beard came out of the
trunk of an old withered tree.

"What are you greeting for, my bonnie
lassie?" said the old man.

"Because my faither wants to marry me,"
said the princess.

"Tell him you'll not marry him till he gets
you a gown and coat and shoes of rashes."*

The princess wiped her eyes, and went back
and told her father she could not marry him till
he got her a gown and coat and shoes of rashes.

* Rushes.

The king was glad to hear her say this, although he did not know how he was to get the things she wanted. But he went to an old witch, and she promised to get them for him in a week if he promised to do something she asked him when she required him. To this the king readily agreed. In a week she brought them and put them on the princess, and they fitted her well. The king then told her she must now marry him, but she ran out crying into the wood, and sat down near the old tree.

The wee old man with the long grey beard came out and said,

" What are you greeting for now, my bonnie lassie ? "

" My faither has got me the gown and coat and shoes o' rashes, and wants me to marry him."

" Tell him," said the wee old man, "you will not marry him till he gets you a gown and coat and shoes of the colour of all the birds of the air."

The princess went and told the king that she could not marry him till he got her a gown, a coat, and shoes of the colour of all the birds of the air. The king went to the old witch again, and she promised to get them for him in a fortnight if he promised to do two things she asked him. To this the king again agreed. She commanded all the birds in the air to come to her, so they all came, and every one gave her a feather. She took the feathers and wove them into a splendid gown and coat and shoes, and they were of all the colours of all the birds in the air.

She brought them to the king and tried them on the princess, and they fitted her beautifully.

The king claimed her for his wife, and asked her to fulfil her promise to marry him.

But she ran out crying to the wood, and sat down beside the hollow tree.

The wee old man with the long grey beard came out of the hollow tree, and said,

"What are you greeting for now, my bonnie lassie?"

She said,

"My faither has got the gown and coat and shoes of the colour of all the birds of the air, and he wants me to marry him."

"Tell him you'll not marry him till he gets you a wedding gown and coat and shoes of woven gold that will be as bright as the sun."

The princess went into the house again, and told the king, her father, that she could not marry him till he got her a wedding gown and coat and shoes of woven gold as bright as the sun.

The king thought this was impossible, but he went to the witch, and she promised to get

them for him in a month if he promised to do
three things for her when she asked him.   The
king consented gladly.

The king agreed to wait for a month, but
this time he was resolved he would not be put
off, and the princess must fulfil her promise
whether she liked it or not.   So he sent invi-
tations to his friends to the wedding at once,
so that they might not say they had got a
fiddler's bidding.   When the month was over
the witch brought the gown and coat and shoes
of woven gold, and they fitted the princess as
the bark does the tree.

" Now," said the king, " you must fulfil your
promise, for I am resolved to be put off no
longer."

She begged and prayed that he would give
her another day.

" I grant you till to-morrow, then, but not a
day longer," said the king.   Then he went off
to give orders for the wedding.   The princess
went out to the wood, and sat down by the
hollow tree, sobbing as if her heart would break.

The wee old man with the long grey beard came out, and said,

" What are you greeting for now, lassie ?"

" The king, my faither, has got me the gown and coat and shoes of the woven gold, and they are as bright as the sun, and I maun marry him to-morrow."

" No, no! You maunna marry your faither. Put on your rashy coat and gown and shoes, tie up your gown of the colour of all the birds, and the coat and shoes to match, and put them in a bundle with the gown and coat and shoes of woven gold, and gang and take service in the king of Scotland's palace. I'll come wi' you and take care of you. Slip out with your bundle when the king's asleep, come here, and you'll see a bird sitting on the tree. That bird will be me."

The princess ran back to the king's house, and tied up her gown and coat and shoes of the colour of all the birds of the air, and her gown and coat and shoes of the woven gold into a bundle. Then she put on her gown and coat and shoes of rushes, and waiting till everybody was asleep, slipped out and went to the wood, where she saw a bird sitting on the hollow tree.

"Here I am," said the bird. "We must be far away before the morning."

So they set off, and were far away before morning.

In the morning the princess could not be found, and the king was wild with rage that all his preparations had been in vain. When he was going to tell his messengers to bid the guests delay their coming, and to tell the cooks to stop the preparations for the wedding dinner, the old witch came in and said,

"Let them go on preparing for the wedding, and let the guests come. A bride will be found when the time comes." Then she said she had something to say privately to the king.

He thought she had some news of the princess, so he took her into a chamber apart.

"Do you remember that you promised to do three things, when I asked you, in return for the gifts I gave you?" said the witch.

"Ye-es," said the king, who had thought very little of his promises in his anxiety to obtain the witch's gifts.

"Well, now, I claim their fulfilment."

The king thought it rather hard that his promises should be mentioned at all when they had failed to accomplish what he wanted. But thinking it would be some trifle of land or privilege that the witch wanted, he said,

"Very well; ask, and I am ready to grant."

"First, then, I wish to try on your last wife's dresses."

"What!" said the king, quite aghast at the vanity of this crooked-looking old woman; then, laughing at the contrast she presented to his late spouse, he said,

"You shall have your wish."

The dresses were brought, and the king left the chamber.

The witch took a sponge and passed it over her face, and she looked a comely middle aged woman. She took off her own gown, and she seemed well formed and shapely. She put on the widest and loosest of the queen's dresses, and though it did not quite fit her at first, she stroked it and nipped it till it sat upon her fairly. Then she told the king to come in.

When the king came in he stared with astonishment, for he recognised in the witch a sweetheart that he had courted and secretly married before he had married the queen.

"'Tis you, Thulla, that has played the witch so long," said he.

"Yes, it is I. See how your wife's dress fits me. Now for my second wish. You must marry me."

"I cannot, I am to marry the princess this very day, or as soon as I can find her."

"You'll never find her till she's married to somebody else. She and her half brother, your son and mine, are far away by this time. Remember, too, the guests are coming, and even I am better than no bride. Besides, a king should not go back from his word."

The king thought after all it was not so bad as it might have been, for he had liked Thulla, who had disappeared when he married the late queen.

" My next wish is that you proclaim me publicly as your queen, and our son as your heir equally with the princess."

The king did not like this condition, but after all it was only justice, so he consented, and immediately began to feel happier than he had done for many a day.

The wedding guests came, and the king and Thulla were publicly married. Then the king formally acknowledged their former private marriage, and declared that Thulla's son was to be equal heir with the princess, if ever they or either of them returned.

Meantime the princess, or Rashycoat, as everybody called her, and her half brother, Thulla's son Jamuck, journeyed on to the city of the king of Scotland. Sometimes he went beside her as an old man with a long grey beard, sometimes he was a bird, but oftenest he walked by her side as a handsome youth, with a face that resembled her father's.

After
a time he
told her
he was her
half brother, and also of
the plot that he and
his mother had arranged
to get the king to ac-
knowledge his private
marriage. Jamuck had
been with the fairies and
learned their secrets; he
said he was not really
transformed into a bird or an old man, but that
he had the power of glamourie, that is, of
making any one who looked on him, see him
exactly as he desired to appear.

When Rashycoat and Jamuck arrived at the
city of the king of Scotland, Jamuck bade Rashycoat go to the king's palace and take service
there, whilst he would also try separately to get
a place near her.

When Rashycoat went to the great entrance

of the palace, she was so much afraid of the great
fierce fellows who stood at the door with their
battle-axes on their shoulders, that she dared
not attempt to go in. So she went round about
till she came to a smaller door, which, from the
clatter of the plates and tongues, she knew to be
the kitchen.

A great feast was being prepared. The head
cook was in a great flurry, because one of her
scullery maids had gone away for a day and had
not returned as she promised, in time to take her
share of the work of the great dinner. The cook
was scolding, and wondering how she was to get
through her work without her due number of
assistants, when Rashycoat came to the door and
asked to take service.

"I suppose you can wash dishes," said the
cook.

Rashycoat, who had often seen the maids in
her father's house do that kind of work, said
she supposed she could.

"Come in then," said the cook, "and earn
your meat."

Rashycoat went in, and doing her best quietly and carefully, became well liked in the kitchen, and had a loft given her to sleep in.

Jamuck went and engaged himself to the hen-wife who supplied the palace with eggs and poultry, so that he often saw Rashycoat when he came with his goods to the kitchen.

After being a month or two in the palace, one Sunday Rashycoat was left alone in the kitchen, as all the other servants had gone to the kirk or to visit their friends.

The bells were still ringing when Rashycoat thought it was time for her to go to the kirk to give thanks to God for her escape from the sin of marriage with her father. But how could she go with this peculiar dress of rashes at which everybody laughed? Suddenly she thought on her bundle. So she ran up to the loft, and dressing herself in her gown and coat and shoes of the colour of all the birds of the air, slipped out and arrived at the kirk after the service had begun. The door-keepers took her to be one of the grand ladies of the court, and as the beautiful figure of the princess in her wonderful dress sailed up the aisle every eye was fixed upon her.

The king's son, the prince of Scotland, could not take his eyes off her sweet face for a moment; and every moment he became deeper and deeper in love with the wonderful stranger.

But before the service was ended, Rashycoat rose and left the kirk, and, hurrying back to her loft, took off her grand dress and put on her gown of rashes.

All the talk of the servants, when they came from the kirk, was about the beautiful lady who had evidently captivated the prince. For, half mad to find out who she was and where she lived, he had offered a great reward to any one who would tell him.

Rashycoat said nothing, but went on carefully with her work; yet the thought of the prince being in love with her gave her great delight, for he was the idol of the people for his handsome face and form, and for his goodness and kindness to all about him.

C

So Rashycoat resolved to try and see him
again, but although she was left in the kitchen
alone the next Sunday, she had work to do that
kept her from going to the kirk. On the second
Sunday the servants insisted on her taking her
day out, so she went, dressed in her gown of
rashes, to see her half-brother Jamuck at the henwife's house. The henwife and her daughter
were at the kirk, so Rashycoat and Jamuck
talked on without restraint.

On the third Sunday, however, Rashycoat was
left alone in the kitchen with nothing to do. So
she ran up to the loft, and dressing herself in her
gown and coat and shoes of woven gold, tripped
off to the kirk.

If she made a commotion in the minds of the
people on the first day, that was nothing to the
sensation she caused as she went up the church
in raiment shining as the sun; while rich as her
apparel was, her incomparable face and form
compelled even the most envious to acknowledge
that never was there a face or a figure that
deserved so well to be royally adorned.

The prince was wild and restless, although
his eyes never left the fair face before him.
The henwife and her daughter, who sat behind
the prince, thought that he need not be quite
so wild about one, who after all, was only a
woman.

As before, Rashycoat rose ere the service
was completed. As she was passing the prince's
seat, the prince determined not to lose sight
of her again, forgot all about his duty to set
a good example to his father's subjects by
reverently waiting till the service was done, and
rose to try and seize Rashycoat's hand as she
passed. But in the agitation of both, he stumbled
or cast himself down at her feet. His hand
rested for a moment on her shoe. Rashycoat,
trembling and fearful, drew out her foot hastily
and fled down the aisle, never pausing till she
reached her loft and exchanged her golden gown
for her ordinary dress of rashes. The prince
pressed the shoe to his lips, and said loud enough
for all those around to hear him, " I will wed the
lady whom this shoe fits, and no other." The hen-

wife and her daughter heard the words, and planned how they might be able to catch the prince. So the henwife set to work, and began clipping the toes and paring the heels of her daughter Every day a little piece more came off the toes and the heels, so that the foot became very small indeed, though the henwife's daughter could not walk from the painful state of her feet.

Jamuck saw all their tricks and heard their plans, and told them to Rashycoat when he went with fowls and eggs to the royal kitchen.

Rashycoat, through constantly thinking about the prince, became as much in love with him as he was with her. So that it was with a thrill of agony that she heard that the prince had proclaimed he would marry the lady whose foot fitted Rashycoat's shoe. Of course nobody would ever think of looking among the scullery maids for the beautiful lady. She listened with a sickening heart to all the stories of how such a one's foot was far too big, how another's was narrow enough but an inch too long, how another was just the right length, but so badly shaped that even by crushing it would not go in ;—at last the terrible news came that the shoe was found, with squeezing, to fit the henwife's daughter, and that she claimed the fulfilment of the prince's promise.

The prince cursed his rashness and impetuosity of temper which had got him into this scrape, but he must keep his word at any cost; so great preparations were made for the marriage of the king's son with the henwife's daughter.

The henwife's daughter showed herself to be proud and vain, and insisted on the prince making his marriage with her as public and grand as possible.

When the day arrived, and flags were flying and bells ringing, Rashycoat went behind the cauldron like to die of disappointed love and grief.

The grand procession took its way from the king's palace to the church. The prince rode on his horse, and the henwife's daughter sat on a pillion behind him.

As they passed out of the palace gateway
a bird that was sitting on the parapet cried
out,

> " Clippëd taes and parëd heels
> Behind the young prince rides,
> But bonny face and pretty foot
> Behind the cau'dron hides."

"What does that bird say ? " said the prince.

" Oh never mind what a filthy clawty bird like
that says," said the henwife's daughter, pressing
the prince's arm.

When they got half-way to the church, they
passed through a narrow street, and up on a
window coronet was the bird again, and again
it said,

> " Clippëd taes and parëd heels
> Behind the young prince rides,
> But bonny face and pretty feet
> Behind the cau'dron hides."

When the bird began, the henwife's daughter
also began speaking loudly to the prince.

So he asked again,

"What is that bird saying ? "

"Why should you mind a clawty bird when your bride is speaking to you?" said the hen-wife's daughter, smiling in a would-be fascinating way in the prince's face.

When they reached the church door there was the bird again, and it cried out so loudly and distinctly, that in spite of all the hen-wife's daughter could do, he heard the bird say,

> "Clippëd taes and parëd heels
> Behind the young prince rides,
> But bonny face and pretty feet
> Behind the cau'dron hides."

The prince pushed the henwife's daughter off the horse, and galloping off soon reached the door of the royal kitchen. Springing from his horse he rushed in and went behind the huge cauldron, where he saw Rashycoat. In spite of her changed dress he knew her at once, and raising her up, he kissed her. He drew the slipper from his bosom. It fitted her as the bark does a tree. Rashycoat pulled the neighbour of it from her pocket and put it on.

" Dress yourself and come with me," said the prince.

Rashycoat went to her loft and speedily returned in her gown and coat of woven gold, and shining like the sun.

The prince set her lovingly upon his horse, and taking his place beside her, rode to the kirk, where they were married, to their own great delight and the satisfaction of all the people.

When they were all at supper, Jamuck, dressed like a prince, came to the palace, and claiming his relationship to Rashycoat, told the prince, king, and all the guests, that Rashycoat was the King of Thulê's daughter.

So everybody was pleased.

After a time Jamuck took his leave of Rashycoat, the prince, and the king, and told them how he had taken the appearance of the bird to prevent the prince being imposed upon.

The prince, who was now more in love with Rashycoat than ever, thanked him warmly, and the two princes vowed to each other enduring friendship.

Then Jamuck returned to Thulê, and in due time succeeded his father as king. Rashycoat and the prince and Jamuck lived happily all their days.

> So now my story's ended
> I hope you're not offended ;
> And if you are offended
> It's more than I intended.´
>
> .

* The northern story-teller usually ends his tale with this or a similar rhyme.

IKOMAR, the wizard-chief, had seized the lands of Rollo, the infant earl of the

Orcades, at his father's death, and when the youth grew up he was landless and almost homeless.

When he was eighteen years old, Rollo challenged Vikomar to the combat, but his blade broke harmlessly on the wizard's crest, and he would have fallen before Vikomar's battle-axe had not some of his late father's friends rallied round him and brought him off unhurt.

## II.

Some time after this, Rollo one evening was sailing alone between the Orcadian Islands, thinking how he might regain his father's seat. Rapt in thought, he suffered his boat to drift far out of its course. The Orcades were hidden by a driving mist; no land was visible, and all night long he tossed upon the resistless restless sea, striving in vain to catch a glimpse of land.

When day-dawn flooded the sky with radiant golden light, he saw an island straight before his vessel's prow. Keeping his course for this, his boat was soon safely beached in a little bay between some cave-worn rocks. Then leaping ashore and fastening his boat he scrambled over the rocks to explore the island.

Soon he reached the foot of a great rocky peak, and stood beside the piles of stone which from their form and colour seemed to have been torn by an earthquake from the face of the mountain. Making his way between these huge stones, which took the form of mighty walls crowned by rude accidental semblances of crouching lions and confused grotesque forms of other animals, he saw before him a great cave pierced into the mountain's side.

When Rollo reached the mouth of this cave he paused an instant, and involuntarily laid his hand on his sword.

"Enter, and fear not," said a pleasant voice. He hastily withdrew his hand from his weapon, and entered into the deep gloom of the cavern.

When his eye had become accustomed to the darkness, he saw that this subterranean mansion had the appearance of a grove of trees suddenly turned to stone; thickly clustered natural columns supported the arched and fretted roof, while arcaded corridors extended in every direction.

Through the arches he could discern a stream which came tumbling wildly down, sparkling in the light, from a rift in the mountain through which it entered the cave. The rocks which hemmed it in were covered with ferns, harebells, oxlips, and nodding violets, which were watered by the spray rising from the torrent as it rushed down the rocks into the dark whirling pool under the level of the cavern floor.

### III.

On looking round he perceived, squatted on the top of one of the huge boulders which strewed the cavern floor, a little dark figure who was eyeing him with steady pertinacity, whilst others moved about through the shadows. Brought up

amongst islands abounding in legends of sea-
maidens, fairies, trolls, gnomes, dwarfs, and sprites,
Rollo believed that some of these mysterious
beings were before him, and he was beginning
to repeat a spell which never failed to discomfit
them, when a hand was laid on his shoulder.
He turned quickly, and beheld a lady, no longer
young, but girt like a queen, with silver gleaming
robe, golden coronal, and embroidered girdle.

Rollo gazed on her with surprise and awe.
She smiled at his amazed stare, and said softly,

" You are weary with your night's vigil on the sea, come and rest."

## IV.

TAKING him by the hand, she led him along a corridor, on the outside of whose rough natural arches the subdued unearthly light gleamed softly on the noisy stream. At the end of this gallery was an upward flight of steps, the whole width of the corridor, and beyond them a screen of sturdy pillars, upon which art had been employed to enrich nature, for the capitals were full of quaint interlacings, and twisting and coiling dragons.

Between these columns they entered a large banqueting hall, in the centre of which was a mighty circular table, carved from the solid rock, with chairs of graven stone grouped round it.

On two sides of the hall were stone seats with embroidered coverings, whilst over them was an arcade filled with storied glass, of divers colours, lighted behind by concealed lamps. At the farther end was the fireplace, corresponding

in size and rich-
ness with the rest
of the apartment,
and having with-
in it a clear fire
burning in a stand
of brazen grill
work.

The table was spread with delicacies more
rare and in vessels more exquisite than were to
be found at a king's table. At the desire of his
hostess, Rollo sat down and began to eat and
drink, and enjoy the rare dainties that graced the
table : marvelling all the while that he had never
before seen or even heard of this island with its
wondrous cave.

After satisfying both hunger and thirst, he
waited for the lady to speak. Her first words
startled him.

" You wish to conquer Vikomar," she said.

" Yes," said Rollo, " 'tis my only chance of
gaining my inheritance."

" You have tried and failed."

" Once! I will try again," he answered eagerly.

She smiled half pityingly as she said,

" No weapon forged of earthborn steel can overcome that man ; he bears a charm given by the evil angel whom he truly serves. You must obtain the fairy sword, Excalibur."

" Half my life I'd give for it, but 'tis impossible; the sword was buried in the southern seas when great King Arthur died."

She said almost fiercely, " To valiant hearts, nothing's impossible, I know where lies the mystic sword. The bards spake truly, a hand did grasp the sword when Bedivere, at Arthur's dying word, cast it o'er the water, and the white mermaiden's arm carried it safe to Phædricon, to this very island, ay, to this very cave."

" To this island! To this very cave!"

" To this island, to this very cave. It lies beneath the centre of this table," said she, striking the great circular rock with the rod she bore in her hand.

"But twenty men could not remove this from its bed," said Rollo.

"No, nor a thousand, and e'en if that were done, the sword would be as far as ever from your eager grasp."

"Then how can it be won?" said Rollo, with passionate eagerness, for the thought of gaining the magic sword had been one of his wild boyhood's dreams, the foundation and the instrument of a hundred airy castles.

"Only," said she, "by a pure heart and a daring one, knit to keen eyes and firm just hands."

"Let me but try," he said.

"Be patient and listen well. Full fifty fathoms beneath this floor is hid a rock-hewn chapel. In its centre aisle is raised the graven tomb to which the weeping queens conveyed the dying Arthur. Upon the tomb his sculptured image lies with arms still wreathed around the diamond sword. For many a year the weeping queens kept watch and guarded Arthur with their holy spells; but now they're gone, and in their place the ghosts of pagans slain hold impious festival around the conquered king. Once the chapel might be gained by easier means, but since an earthquake tore the labouring hill there is no entrance from the upper air, save by the channel of the brawling stream which sinks beneath yon corridor."

" I'll dive and bring the sword at once," said Rollo.

"Stay! to attempt it now is certain death. The nightly rains which feed the mountain stream choke up the channel and leave no space for air; when sunset comes the stream is at its lowest, and even then you will not find your breath till you are gasping ; for half the way is full from floor to roof."

" My sword and dagger, they will be enough ? "

" Ay truly, and too much for your dear life ; for know, the pagan ghosts that haunt that lower world will aim their moonbeam swords against your breast and hurl their spectre javelins at your eyes; but fear them not, those cannot do you harm ; but could they lay their fleshless fingers on an earthly sword, 'twere instant death to you. Or if you bear an ill wish in your heart against a fellow mortal, I pray you go not down, for though you may return, the task will be far harder. So cast out every speck of malice from your soul, and purge your heart as far as in you lies from all unholy thoughts and vain desires. Soon I shall send my music trolls to give you sleep till sunset." As she uttered these last words she disappeared behind the screen of columns.

Rollo paced up and down, alternately praying for help in his bold emprise and examining his heart in order to fulfil the injunctions of Chryseja, his strange hostess. By and

by a strain of weird quaint music reached his ears
—ineffably sweet it was, unlike anything he had
ever heard before. A mantle of dreams seemed
to be woven by unseen fingers around him, in
time to the cadence of the music. Soon he
dropped on one of the couches by the side of
the wall, and was instantly fast asleep.

## V.

At sunset he was awakened by Chryseja.

" The sun is setting and the time has come,"
she said.

" I'm ready," said Rollo, springing up and
grasping his sword.

" Nay, do not buckle on your sword ; you
remember my warning."

He laid down his weapons and threw off his
tunic. She scanned him narrowly, then she said,

" You are not afraid of the risk you run?"

" To win Excalibur I'd dare a thousand such."

" My hope goes with you," she said. "'Tis now
the likeliest hour. The pagan ghosts at sunset

fall asleep and wake at midnight to perform their awful mysteries.    Come."

She led him into the corridor, and through the arches to the rocky brink of the dark whirling and surging pool into which the stream descended roaring, but bringing with the cool breeze of sunset.    Ascending an immense flat-topped rock on which lay a coil of thin but tough rope made from the sinews of the wild deer : this rope she proceeded to bind round his waist, saying in explanation,

"'Tis for your return, for never would you see this light again without its aid, for 'twould be hopeless to attempt to swim upward through the dreadful sweeping cataract by which you must descend.    Remember, when you have gained the sword and reached again the teeming channel whence the waters come, bind again this rope around your waist and give three equal pulls. I shall know the signal ; and my little men shall drag you swiftly through the dangerous chasm."

"I'm ready, and will remember," said Rollo, preparing to dive.

"Stay one instant; dive straight for the centre of the pool, and let the swirling current suck you in; and now God speed you."

Rollo bent and kissed her hand; then drawing a deep breath, he shot clean and sharply into the centre of the troubled waters and disappeared. For an instant the rope waveled idly and then began to run out with great rapidity, for about fifty beats of Chryseja's heart; then the rope moved more slowly till it was all run out.

Chryseja lifted her eyes and said fervently, "Thank heaven he has escaped the jagged rocks." She then sat down on the rock beside the iron ring to which the rope was fastened, and taking a silver whistle from her bosom, blew loud and shrilly. The sound was echoed in numberless corridors. Instantly from rocky clefts, from under brackens and nodding wild flowers, from caves under the very waterfall, appeared a host of little men and women. None of them were more than a cubit high, but their eyes sparkled with more than earthly intelligence. They were clad in tender green of various shades, and

wore pointed caps of various colours, which
blended so harmoniously that it seemed as if
a garden of flowers had suddenly been endowed
with life.

They gathered in circles round Chryseja, and
knelt with their faces towards her.

"Thanks, thanks, my little friends," she said,
"for your prompt appearance. Now you must
do me a service. A son of that royal line who
always loved your race has dived to gain the magic
sword Excalibur, and upward you must drag him
through the cataract." A chorus of bell-like voices
jingled out, "We will! we will!" and seizing the
rope, the little people began to pull.

"Stay! stay! not yet," cried Chryseja, "or he
will be lost."

They instantly let go the rope and knelt again
around her.

'Hark, Puckæron," said she, "whilst I instruct
you. Do you stand at the edge of the rock, and
you, Delilith, at the ring. Nomanoë must take
the middle place, and all my other friends must
take a hold as they find space between. When

you, Puckæron, feel the rope's first jerk, let Delilith untie it from the ring, and when the third signal is given, drag it, and fly as if the lightning chased you till I cry, Hold!"

The pigmies arranged themselves on the great rock as she desired them, and waited eagerly for the signal.

## VI.

WHEN Rollo dived into the black swirling pool, he was instantly caught by the current that whirled round the almost perpendicular tunnel which formed the outlet to the stream, and was carried swift as a shooting star down in utter darkness through the black tearing and rushing water which filled the passage from floor to roof. Down, down he went, buffeted and lashed by the horribly roaring water. Still down, till his heart throbbed and his head was like to burst; then, when it seemed impossible any longer to hold his breath, he was shot in a lower rocky basin, which received the torrent as it came spouting from the tunnel. Rising to the surface, he drew a deep

breath, and allowed himself to drift on the surface
of the pool till he reached a rock on its edge.

Loosening the rope and looking back, the
sight was even more fearful than the actual experience had been. A dim light struggling through
some rocky cleft showed out the jagged, teeth-
like, and dripping rocks, with a vague horrible
indistinctness. From the mouth of the cavern
from which he had emerged the tortured waters
came spouting, foaming, and roaring with deafen-
ing din into the pool, which seemed to boil with
fury, while the spray, rising in clouds, aided this
illusion.

Clinging to the rock on which he had landed,
he made the rope fast to a jutting peak, and proceeded to follow the course of the torrent, which
was to lead him to the chapel where the body of
King Arthur lay. The way was tortuous, slippery,
and full of difficulty and danger. The waters
leaving the pool leaped down in cascades, while
oftentimes the rocks which formed the roof sunk
so low as almost to meet the water, whilst here and
there a jagged inverted peak dipped in, causing

the waves to chafe and foam more angrily as they dashed against it.

Creeping cautiously along the side, sometimes up to the neck in water, sometimes swimming with the current, clambering over rocks and through crevices to avoid the waterfalls, he at length saw before him a large smooth surface of rock, in which was an arched doorway carved round about with coiling, twisting, and interlacing dragons. A flight of steps led down from this door to the water, which foamed against the steps, and then went thundering into a chasm of utter darkness.

As Rollo sat for a few minutes to rest on the steps, he gazed anxiously up at the arch within whose portal the most fearful and perilous part of his adventure was, he believed, to take place. There he was not to encounter mere physical dangers, but the mysterious beings of another world. Without armour, without sword, without even a dagger, the appalling helplessness of his case made him shrink with dismay : and for an instant he thought to flee the dreaded place.

But the thought of possessing the Enchanted Sword, and of winning his birthright by its aid, made him start up determined to achieve the purpose of his descent at all hazards.

Commending himself to heaven, he walked boldly up the steps. Lifting the iron latch and pushing up the door, which opened noiselessly, he entered the fate-fraught chapel. The door swung as noiselessly back to its place, and closed of its own accord.

## VII.

ALTHOUGH in reality the chapel was but dimly lighted, the contrast of the illuminated building with the almost utter darkness in which he had been so long, dazzled him. Shading his eyes with his hand, he gazed earnestly forward. He saw that the chief light proceeded from the centre of the farther end, where, beyond the altar, on a mighty pedestal of rock, a warlike figure of gigantic size was placed. Its right hand was fiercely raised, and was grasping a ponderous mace or hammer. In its left hand, fashioned as a drink ing cup, was a human skull set with gold, and having the grinning teeth and sightless sockets conspicuously displayed.

The war-god's head was thrown back, his nostrils were distended, and his teeth shone white against his long floating red beard. His eyes gleamed, and, burning in their sockets, shed rays of light over the whole length of the building. It was this light that, glaring on him when he entered, had for the moment dazzled Rollo. He soon perceived that not only were the eyes luminous, but that the whole figure was light-giving, though in a less degree.

Turning his gaze by an effort from this figure, Rollo saw that the aisles were filled with shadowy sleeping warriors. These men,—strong, muscular, and fierce, with rough wild locks and wing-like beards, were all armed for combat,—each right hand grasping, even in sleep, keen sword, deadly battle-axe, or bristling mace. Drinking horns, overturned pitchers, bowls and beakers, lay scattered about. Among the warriors lay sleeping, stark and strong wolf and stag hounds, whose

long white fangs shone out of the indistinct light
of the aisles.

Under the centre of each arch was a tripod of
brass, which sparkled in the light from the burning
incense within it. At the foot of each tripod lay
a fair-haired youth, attendant spirit of the fire.

In spite of the fierce attitude of the colossal
war-god at the remote end, a most unearthly
silence prevailed ; the roar of the outside water
was unheard, and a fearful and oppressive stillness
shrouded everything within the chapel. There
was not a sound save the beating of Rollo's heart,
which beat more wildly when, far up the chapel
and almost at the feet of the fire-eyed god, he
descried the tomb on which lay the sculptured
effigy of the Christian king.

Rollo advanced firmly up the centre aisle,
looking neither to the right nor left, till, on reach-
ing the sepulchre of King Arthur, he saw that the
arms were lightly crossed above the sword
Excalibur. Then glancing quickly round the
chapel upon the host of sleeping warrior-shades,
he tried to draw the sword and its sheath from

beneath the arms of the sculptured figure. But
the instant that the sword began to move the
sleeping ghosts awoke, and starting up, thronged
madly and fiercely against him ; like waves they
came on as if to overwhelm him. Their red beards
waved, their eyes gleamed with rage, their armour
glanced. Brandishing flashing swords, glittering
axes, and gleaming spears, they came on and
rained their spectral blows on Rollo's head with an
absolute absence of sound which struck cravingly
and with horror on the ear.

He still pulled at the enchanted sword, and
when fairly within his grasp, he drew it from its
scabbard and whirled it round his head in the faces
of the threatening spectres, who gave way before
it. As he walked towards the door by which he had
entered, the faces of the warriors became more
and more despairing. When his hand was almost
on the latch, he turned and looked up the church.
Gazing over and beyond the host of spectral
warriors, he beheld the vast luminous figure writhing with impotent rage, striving, as it seemed, to
burst from some all-powerful though hidden spell

which bound its feet to the pedestal. As Rollo
turned to depart, a look of fearful and unutterable

anguish passed across the countenance of the
mighty figure of light, and it sank powerless on
the seat; its light faded, flickered, then suddenly

shooting up again, wrapped the whole figure in a
sheet of flame.   There was a sound like a thunder
peal, and then all was blackest darkness, while the
chapel swayed, rocked, and trembled, as if stirred
by a mighty earthquake.   Rollo pressed the latch
to pass out of the chapel : to his alarm and horror
the door resisted all his efforts to open it, and
would nor stir.   He was shut in that hall of grisly
dead ; the spectres which he could not see, he felt
were crowding round him, the air was stifling, and
his whirling brain peopled the air with shapes a
thousand times more frightful than his eyes had
seen.   They were upon him; he felt their venomous
breath on his cheek, in his throat.   His flesh was
creeping and his hair on end with horror.

\*　　　\*　　　.\*　　　\*　　　\*

Was he becoming mad ? surely a light was
now dawning over the chapel altar ?

Yes, in the chancel there was a light which
revealed—in place of the war-god and his grisly
train—a pale form hanging from a cross.   Before
it knelt seven queens golden crowned and clad
in whitest samite.   From their lips arose a strain
of heavenly music.

Rollo fell on his knees and bowed his head in prayer. The music ceased. He heard the roar of the torrent. The chapel was dark again, but the door was open!

He passed out, and sinking on his knees upon the steps, he offered up his earnest thanks for the success of his enterprise. Filled with an over-flowing joy, he proceeded up the subterranean channel of the torrent, amidst rocks and roaring water, to the spot where he had left the rope, on which and the help of heaven depended all prospects of ever seeing again the light of day.

## VIII.

CHRYSEJA and her pigmy attendants waited by the upper pool for Rollo's signal. More than an hour had passed, and still the rope was motionless save for the undulations caused by the water as it alternately dragged at, and released it. Chryseja's eyes were fixed on the place where the rope disappeared in the deep black pool. Her little men sat in a long row on the immense flat rock, patiently waiting for the signal.

The steady undulation of the rope pained Chryseja, who began to fear that Rollo had been swallowed up by some of the abysses which abounded in his path, or that he had fallen a victim, like many others, to the vigilance of the spectral guardians of the magic sword.

"Surely," she said, pacing hurriedly backwards and forward on the rocky platform, "I was not deceived, the boy bears a pure and noble heart; but if"—and she shuddered as she spoke—"he carried a knife, a bodkin even, to that fearful hall, his life may now be ebbing on the war-god's altar."

The light of day, which at best came but scantily into that rocky cavern, was now almost gone, but in its stead were numbers of sweet-smelling torches grouped around the massive natural columns which upheld the roof. As daylight altogether disappeared, the strong lights and shadows (constantly changing as the leaping and writhing flames of the torches were swayed by conflicting currents of air) brought out in fierce relief, or doomed to utter blackness, the

stone fantasies and grotesque shapes of the
colossal rocks ; and the weird fantastic grandeur
of the place became more apparent.

With her eyes still fixed on the rope, Chryseja
continued her walk, becoming more and more
anxious and excited as the hours passed without
the signal being given.

Just as despair was beginning to creep into
her heart, the rope was sharply strained for an
instant—it was loosened—the signal was repeated!

"Quick, my little ones," she cried. "You
have, I see, Delilith, untied it from the ring. Be
ready all to fly like storm-fiends when I cry,
Away! The breath of noble youth is in your
hands. You're ready!" With eyes fixed on their
mistress, and with firm sinewy hands grasping the
rope, the dwarfs bowed their heads to signify that
all was ready.

The third signal was given!

"Away!" she cried, and away they sped like
lightning over the rock, disappearing in the
corridor immediately opposite.

Chryseja stood on the brink of the pool and

watched the cord as it flew by. " Now heaven
be good to him," she prayed, "who shoots through
that dark watery chasm; from jagged rocks and
all unwrecked-of dangers, oh! keep him scatheless
still."

The rope continued to fly past.

And now—three knots placed at a little distance from the lower end, burst out of the water.
Her silver whistle sounded shrilly out, and her
voice rang through the corridor, along which
sped the little men, bidding them stay. At once
they stopped, and the same moment the upward
pointed hands, and then the face of Rollo, appeared
above the water.

She seized the rope, and gently towed the
half-stunned youth to the side, and assisted him
to climb the rock.

" Is it well with you ?" she asked, as he sank
down at her feet.

A look of happiness passed over his wet pale
face, and he bowed his head and pointed to the
sword bound at the hilt to his waist, and upheld
at the point by his left hand.

"It is Excalibur," he gasped, with a triumphant smile.

She unloosed the cord, and led him to the great hall. "In yonder chamber," she said, pointing to an archway hung with silken curtains, "you will find fresh raiment. But first drink this." She poured some warm fragrant liquor into a golden cup. As he drank it, a delicious glow went through his frame, which had been chilled by his long battle with the waters.

He went into the chamber, and after a little time came back into the hall clad in a rich dress, and with armour that shone like the sun. At his side was Excalibur, hanging by a belt enriched with golden twisting dragons. Chryseja surveyed him with a pleasant look, and said, "This is as it should be; the enchanted armour is wedded to the magic sword. Be brave, and you will be invincible. Now come and eat."

After satisfying his appetite, Rollo fell asleep on one of the couches. When he awoke it was morning.

When he was about to depart, Chryseja accompanied him to the entrance of the cave, and said, as she bade him farewell,

"Go forth and conquer, Vikomar shall fall beneath your sword, and your birthright shall again be yours. The magic sword will lead you to the southern lands; be just and fear not, fare thee well!"

## IX.

As his boat sped over the water, Rollo turned to look at the island he had left. Instead of an island he only saw thick gathering clouds, in the forms of men, women, horses, and chariots. As they crossed the sky, Rollo saw that what he took for clouds was Odin and his warriors hurling

along through wreathing mists and waving sky foam. On they sped till they faded from his sight. "They have lost the sword they were guarding," said Rollo, "and now the old Norse gods are seeking another home."

Turning his face again to his vessel prow he saw his own Orcadian isles before him, and in due time he safely reached them.

The words of Chryseja were fulfilled. Rollo easily overcame the wizard-chief Vikomar, and regained his own inheritance. Then he sailed throughout the islands, righting those who were wronged and punishing the oppressors. His courage, justice, and unfailing success drew all the brave hearts to his standard. When there was peace all over the islands, Rollo and his men set sail for the Southern lands, where cruel men lorded it over their weaker brethern. After carrying the terror of his arms to the very gates of Paris, he founded the Kingdom of Normandy in the year of our Lord 912.

Rollo became renowned for his wisdom. And so enduring is the fame of his justice that even to this day his presence is invoked by those who are oppressed.*

In the year A.D. 1066 William of Normandy, the descendant of Rollo, conquered England, and the blood of the Orcadian Earl rules Britain to this day.

Excalibur has again disappeared, and since Rollo's time no man has seen it. When the man who is fit to wield it appears, the sword, it is said, will again be found.

---

* This is called the Clameur de Haro. The inhabitant of Normandy or the Channel Isles, who believes himself unjustly oppressed and knows of no other means of escaping from the rapacity of his adversary, goes down on his knees, and lifting his eyes to heaven cries, "Ha! Roul (or Rollo), to my aid, my prince;" and such is the power of the name of the Orcadian Earl in this day, that the oppressor never dares to persist.

the Green Island there was once a little lad called Jack, who lived with his mother in a cottage which stood near a wooded glen. In this glen was a stream which in some places ran over little stones, and dashed against big ones; at others, it leaped down high rocks to the dark pools below.

One day his mother sent Jack to the Wooded Glen to gather sticks, for her stock of fuel was nearly done. He set off at once, and soon gathered a good bundle of nice dry twigs.

He was about to return when he heard a bird sing in the leaves over his head. There were plenty of other birds singing, but of them he had taken no heed; this one, however, sang so sweetly and cheerily, that he looked up to see the singer. It sat on a branch far from the ground, and appeared so tame that he thought he should like to go a little nearer.

Climbing up, he reached the branch, and discovered that the bird had a long ribbon tied to one of its feet. Jack caught hold of the end of this ribbon, thinking he could easily draw the bird towards him; but giving a little nod and a chirrup, it flew away, far above the trees, and disappeared on the other side of the glen.

Jack, who had kept fast hold of the ribbon,

was astonished to find it lengthen, and lengthen, as the bird flew. He waited to feel the tug when the bird came to the end of its tether, but no such thing happened.

Said Jack to himself, "The bird is at the other end of the ribbon, however, and if I wind it up I shall be sure to catch the bird." So he took the ribbon in his teeth and slid down the tree.

When he reached the ground beside his bundle of sticks, he looped the end of the ribbon round his left foot, and began to wind the rest of it round his left hand.

He never saw such a ribbon ; sometimes it was green, sometimes blue, sometimes pink, and sometimes all the colours of the rainbow.

As he continued to wind and admire it, he heard the jingle and tinkle of bells. Every moment the sound came nearer. At last he saw, coming through the trees on the other side of the glen, a very lovely little Princess, with long shining hair, and having a glittering crown on her head. She was mounted on a pretty white horse, and it was the silver bells which were hanging at its mane that Jack had heard.

The princess rode down to the water's edge, and Jack trembled when he saw that the other end of his ribbon was fastened to one of the hind legs of her horse.

In a very sweet but firm voice, the princess said,

"What are you doing with my horse's ribbon ? Bring it here to me."

"I am coming," said Jack, and he began to step from one stone to another, to reach the other side of the stream. He had got rather more than half-way across, when his right foot slipping, he threw up his left hand to balance himself, forgetting that his left foot was fastened to it by the ribbon. Of course he jerked his foot from under him and would have fallen into the water, had not the princess, at the same moment, touched her horse, which, spreading a pair of gossamer wings that Jack had not before perceived, rose swiftly in the air carrying Jack up with it.

It was very nice thus to be saved from a duck-
ing, but Jack was both astonished and afraid,
when he found that the princess and the horse
continued to fly swiftly through the air. The
ribbon by which he was upheld was so slight, that
at first he expected every moment to find it giving
way. When he found that, slight as it was, it was
well able to bear his weight, and that the loop
beneath his foot supported him without fatigue, he
ventured to look down to the world he was so
rapidly leaving.

Although it was only a little while since they
started, the earth was already fading from his sight.
He could just see the sparkle of the sun on the
water, everything else was lost in the haze of
distance.

Swifter and swifter flew the horse, and Jack
began to enjoy the lightning-like speed of his
flight. They rose till the earth looked like a
distant star; ever as they went meteors flew by, on
which wild-eyed spirits sat urging on their fiery
steeds with shouts and furious gestures; comets
with trains of hazy long-haired beings were passed

and left far behind. In the distance appeared stars a thousand times larger than our sun, each whirling on in its course under the guidance of a great radiant-eyed angel.

All the air was full of most delightsome music, "for not the smallest orb but in his motion like an angel sings, still quiring to the young-eyed cherubims."

The fairy steed no longer seemed to rise, and they floated on in a delightful golden atmosphere of soft all-pervading light. Soon they came in sight of a wondrous land, with golden sands and rocks of shimmering pearl, which were washed by a rippling pale green sea.

The sky over the wondrous land was spanned by two arches of light which looked like rainbows at a distance; but when Jack came nearer he saw they were made up of countless thousands of bright-faced, golden-haired youths with wings of sheeny golden green, full of deep purply blue eyes like those of peacocks' feathers.

The horse glided on and descended in front of a city with walls of clear crystal and gates of ivory.

When they came up to one of these gates Jack saw shining in diamonds these words :—

ENTER · BOLDLY · DO · NOT · FEAR ·
GREAT · DELIGHTS · AWAIT · YOV · HERE ·

When he read this, he ran forward and pushed at the gate with his right hand, but he could not move it.

"Press it with your other hand," said the Princess.

Jack touched the gate lightly with his left hand, round which the ribbon was wound, and the mighty gates rolled back and disclosed a street so wide, that on it a hundred chariots might be driven abreast without touching. This street ran from the gate straight to the centre of the city, where stood the Moonbeam Palace of Ædonias, the king of the Wondrous Land.

The road was paved with emeralds so transparent that Jack could see far down into the centre of the earth.

On each side of the street were beautiful gardens, in which were crystal hills, grottoes, singing fountains, waterfalls, and lakes with delightful islands. Boats of pearl, with curling prows and silken sails, skimmed along the lakes, while the sounds of soft music crept over the waters, as the Ædonians, in their boats, played and sang in the soft golden light which shimmered over this enchanting land.

Others of the Ædonians, as the inhabitants were called, sported in the gardens, or in the grottoes and caves, which were as light as day, for all the rocks in the wondrous land were of clear crystal. The trees and flowers were likewise all transparent, though of varied colours, and Jack could see the sap rising in the stems and the life moving and working in the leaves.

What surprised him was, that there seemed to be no houses. The Fairy Princess explained to him that these were not needed, for here the sun never scorched, rain never wetted, cold never chilled.

"Even the Moonbeam Palace," she continued, "for all its thousand pillars and shining domes, is not a house, for the king's sapphire throne is placed

F

on the top of its loftiest dome. The great
reception room is the open sky, shaded only by
the two rainbows of fair winged sprites."

" Is not the king lonely sitting by himself so
high ? " said Jack.

" No, he is not ; he knows his people and they
know him ; he hears each word they speak, and
they hear him, though you cannot ; then these
rainbow angels, with their ever-varying songs and
wings of quivering light, are brave companions.
Besides, from his high throne the king can look
on every part of his dominions, and see each one
of all his happy people, and they are glad to
have upon them the eye of one whose constant
thought is all for their delight."

Jack spent many pleasant days in this enchanting city ; he rode in the gold and ivory
chariots, sailed in the ships of pearl, sported in
the grottoes, and played beside the singing
fountains in the gardens of transparent trees
and flowers.

Everybody here seemed to wish to see everybody else happier than himself, nobody pushed

into the best place, but each one rejoiced, when, by giving up anything, he was able to add to another's enjoyment.

Jack was delighted with the attentions he received, and at first refused occasionally to take the best seat or accept the rare things which all so freely offered him.

After a time, however, he began to regard these things as his right, and as no one ever refused him anything, he imagined himself a very important personage.

None of the Ædonians ever remembered being in any land but this, and Jack thought his former experience as an inhabitant of the Green Island rendered him of greater consequence than any of them; he therefore secretly thought he ought to be their king.

Wherever he had gone as yet, he had always been accompanied by the Fairy Princess, and the ribbon had never left his hand; now, however, he resolved to get out of his leading-strings.

One evening he told her that he wished to remove the ribbon; she earnestly desired

him for his own safety to let it remain. Jack,
suspicious that she wished to keep him controlled,
said,

"I want to ascend the Moonbeam Palace and
stand beside the sapphire throne, that I may see all
the king's dominions."

"Your eyes are too dim, you could not see a
thousandth part," said she.

"I think I can see as far as anybody else,"
said he, very much hurt. "Come, let me
try."

"Up the highest dome I will not go, nor will
you, if you are wise : but I will take you to its
terraced base, whence you may have a goodly
prospect."

"Well, let us go to the palace roof at least,"
said Jack.

The horse carried the Princess and Jack to the
top of the palace, and they alighted on the terraced
hanging garden, which formed a base from which
the highest dome rose like a mighty moon-cloud.
At its top was placed the sapphire throne of King
Ædonias.

Seeing that a great number of stairs ran up
from the place on which they stood to the very
footstool of the throne, Jack thought he could
now dispense with the fairy's further assistance.
He slipped the ribbon off his hand, and was about
to throw it back to the Princess when it shrivelled
up and disappeared.

" Unhappy boy, what have you done?" said she.

" Done ! I have gained my freedom, and now I
will be king, for like people, like king ; and as no
one refuses my wish in this land, I am sure the
king will, like the rest, give me his most honour-
able seat."

"You are right," she said, "in saying ' like king
like people,' and you are free to sit upon the throne
if you are fit. Oh! Jack, beware of pride ; you are
not wise enough to be the king of this fair land ;
come down with me to the city before it be too
late."

"Never !" said Jack ; "I am not to be so lightly
turned from my purpose. How beautiful everything looks from this terraced roof, and how
enchanting it will be when I reach yonder throne

See! the rainbows are quite near, and almost touch the highest point."

" Too near they'll prove for you, I fear; will you not come back with me ? "

" No," said Jack; "you brought me from the Green Island without asking my leave, so now I stay here without yours."

She continued to urge him. Jack ordered her rudely to begone and to trouble him no more.

The Princess, giving him a look of pity, said as she flew away on her horse,

" Beware, oh, beware the morning light."

Jack turned himself and began to ascend the steps that led up to the throne. After he had mounted to some height, he saw that the throne was far larger than it looked from the roof beneath, and that upon it sat a vast dim form which shone like a sculptured moonbeam against the deep blue of the midnight sky. The features of the great king he saw not, for his moonbeam mantle was wrapped thick round his head. Yet he perceived two starry eyes piercing the cloud-like drapery and sparkling like stars through the trail of a comet.

Jack was filled with awe as he gazed; his head drooped, and he fixed his eyes on the steps as he continued to climb. Then he tried to restore his failing courage by muttering aloud,

"Nobody has denied me anything here; I know the king will not refuse me; of course I do

not really want to take his seat against his will,
I only wish to look over all the Wondrous
Land."

Some hours passed as he alternately climbed
and rested. He was getting very tired. "Strange,"
he thought, " I never knew what it was to be weary
while I carried that ribbon, but anybody would
be tired climbing to such a height. How close
the rainbows seem ! I can see the light shining in
the angels' eyes and the quivering of their wings.
It is almost dawn."

He was now at the bottom of the last flight of
steps. He paused to take breath, then, as he
began again to ascend, day dawned, and the nether
sky was all aflame with golden light. Then the
rainbow angels began to hail the day-spring with
delightful songs.

Jack was enraptured and thrilled with the
music ; he could not move at first, then he began
to mount, keeping time to the music with his feet,
saying as he went, " The Fairy wanted to frighten
me with her ' Beware the morning light,' for now
it is morning, and here I am at the very throne

itself, and as there seems to be only a mist upon it, I may take possession."

As he stepped forward to seat himself, the songs of the angels ceased.

With the last note every one bowed his head, and spreading out his mighty glistering wings swept them in till they covered his face.

The first breath of the wind raised by their wings blew aside the moonbeam mantle from the great king, and Jack saw a face of such awful majesty looking down upon him, that he was about to kneel adoringly, but ere his knees touched the pavement, the full force of the whirl-wind raised by the angels' wings was upon him.

Whirled like a feather from before the throne, Jack was carried far beyond the limits of the wondrous land. He began to fall! fall! fall! till his senses failed him.

When he came to himself, he was lying beside his bundle of sticks in the wooded glen of the Green Island.

Years have passed. Jack is very humble now. He still looks out for the Fairy Princess, or for a

glimpse of the magic ribbon. He believes he shall
see her again; when he does so, he is resolved
that she shall find him as humble and obedient as
it is possible for her to desire.

**R**AB was a farm-servant, strong in the body, but rather weak in the head. He was a terrible glutton, and never seemed to know when to stop when he had once begun eating.

Like wiser men, Rab fell in love, and although he did not lose his appetite, he lost a good deal of time, sighing and thinking about Jenny, whom he had seen in the kirk, and who was the daughter of a neighbouring small farmer.

After staring many Sundays at Jenny without daring to open his mouth to speak to her, he at last summoned up courage to ask Jock, his neighbour-servant, who was courting Jenny's sister, Jean, to take him with him on the next Friday when he went to see his lass.

"Man, Rab," said Jock, "I wad be gled to tak' you wi' me, but you're sic' an awful eater, that Jean would never speak to me again, if she kent you were a freen o' mine."

"Ah," said Rab slyly, "I've thocht on that, and we'll manage fine if you jist tramp * on my foot when ye think I've eaten enough at supper-time."

"Well, I'll tak' ye wi' me if you promise that, and mind when they press you to tak' some mair, as they will dae oot o' politeness, tell them you've had great superfluity, for that's what the gentry say, and Jenny will never look at you unless you're geyan well bred."

"Tak' my word for't, Jock," said Rab, "I'll be as mim an' modest as a lass when her lad's

* Tread.

looking at her. 'Supper floority.' Man, that's a gran' word."

"Superfluity," said Jock, correcting him.

"Weel, I said 'Superfluidy.'"

When next Friday night came round, Jock and Rab washed and dressed themselves, and took the road for the house of their sweethearts.

Jock was a favourite both with the old folks and the young, and Rab was well received for his sake; he was introduced to Jenny, and if he thought her bonny in the kirk, he thought her bonnier than ever in her father's house, and he could not keep his eyen off her.

After a lot of courting and laughing and daffing, Jean and Jenny spread the supper on the big table in the kitchen, and when the auld father had said the grace, they all set to work on the victuals.

Rab was tremendously hungry, and his eyes sparkled when he saw so much fit for eating before him. But he had scarcely taken in half-a-dozen mouthfuls, when the big dog which was under the table pressed heavily on Rab's foot.

Thinking it was the signal agreed upon, and that Jock had pressed his foot, Rab with a sigh pushed back his plate, and declared he could not eat any more. Jock was surprised, and told him to continue a little longer, and father, mother, Jean, and Jenny, all pressed him to eat. But Rab was prepared for this show of politeness, and said,

"No, no thank you, I have had great Flipperty Flapperty;" for he had forgot the fine word.

They all laughed at this, and Rab laughed too, although it was no laughing matter to him to see everybody eating and never a bite coming into his own watering jaws.

When the supper things were being stowed away, Rab kept his eyes about and saw where they were put, for as Jock and he were to sleep in the house that night, he resolved to make up for his abstinence at supper-time, when the folk went to bed.

Then all drew round the fire and told stories, sang songs, and guessed riddles; and they finished up grandly with "Bab at the bowster."

Rab, while he sat gazing at Jenny's blithe face, forgot his hunger, but as soon as their sports and daffing were over, and Jock and he had retired to their room in the loft, his stomach reminded him of its awful emptiness.

"Jock, said he, I'm gaun to slip doon to the pantry. I ken whar they pat the big pie."

"Bide a wee till a's quate, it's ower syin tae gang doon yet. And I think, as I'm better aquant wi' the hoose than you, it wad be better if I gang and bring something up to you," said Jock.

After resisting Rab's arguments for immediate action, and waiting till all was still in the kitchen, Jock went softly down the stair, and got to the awmrie in the kitchen. But he could find no pie there. The only thing he could lay hands on was a big bowl full of sowans.*

"This is better than nothing," said Jock, "and Rab's unco fond o' sowans when he canna get onything better."

He crept carefully up the pitch dark staircase, and entered a room opening on the stair-head.

* "Sowans," meal seeds steeped in water.

"Here, Rab," he whispered. "It's only sowans, but it was a' that I could get."

There was no reply, but a very loud snore.

"What, fa'en asleep already? or are you only schaemin', efter I've ta'en a' this trouble," said Jock.

As the conviction that Rab was shamming sleep dawned on Jock, he got angry, and said in an impressive whisper,

"If ye dinna sit up this meenit and tak' the bowl oot ma haund, I'll poor it doon yer thrapple."

No attention being paid to this threat, he said, "I've gi'en ye warnin', so here it goes. Yince, twice, thrice," and he emptied the bowl on the face of the sleeper. Choking and spluttering, the guidman of the house awoke and sat up in bed,—for it was he that had got the sowans in his face,—and coughed, and better coughed, till he wakened his auld wife, who was sleeping by his side.

"What's the matter wi' ye, guidman?"

"As syare's daeth I dinna ken. But I hae had an awfu' dream. I thocht that hole i' the thack *

---

* Thatch.

had broken again, and the water cam' doon on ma heed. An' it's true eneuch, but it tastes unco like sowans."

"It's a fine dry nicht, it couldnae be the rain comin' in; ye maun hae gi'en a bit bock in yer sleep after yer heavy supper," said the auld guid-wife.

"Maybe that's it," said the guidman, wiping his face and composing himself to sleep.

Meanwhile, Jock, finding his mistake, tried the other door on the stair-head. There he found Rab, with hunger in his voice, asking eagerly what he had brought. Jock told him of his mishap, and how he was only able to bring sowans.

"Ye gaed to the awmrie," said Rab. "It wisnae the awmrie whar they put the pie; it was in the pantry jist ootside the kitchen door. Ah reckon ah can fin' meat oot as ready as you can, for a' ye think ye're sae clever." So saying, he slipped down the stair and found his way without mishap to the pantry.

He thought he would just take a mouthful or two and slip back to bed, but every bite seemed to be only a fresh whet to his devouring appetite.

He finished the pie and felt hungrier than ever. He laid hold of a shank of mutton, and tore away at it with his teeth.

By this time the big dog seemed to think Rab had been long enough in the pantry, so he came sniffing and gurring at the door.

"Puir Towser, puir auld fallow," said Rab, between the bites at the mutton.

As soon, however, as Towser heard the voice of the stranger, he set up a loud and vicious bark.

"Guidness," said Rab, "I maun get back to my bed. It'll never dae to be catched here."

"Puir Towser, puir auld man," said he, opening the door a little.

But Towser, proof against his blandishments, rushed furiously at his legs, and he was glad to shut the door hastily.

Towser was now fairly roused, and seemingly resolved to rouse the house, for he leaped at the door, and barked with all his might.

Rab heard the voice of the guidman answering the cries of the various men and women of the household.

"I canna face them," said Rab; "I maun get out at the window. It's sma' eneuch, but gor I can try." He got up on a stool and pushed his head and half his body through the narrow window. Then he gave a mighty push at the stool to send his body quite through, but the stool upset and went from his feet, so that having nothing to push against, and nothing to lay hold of with his hands, he stuck fast.

When the guidman with a candle in the one hand, and a poker in the other, opened the pantry door, and he and his men and women folk looked in, they saw only a pair of legs kicking wildly in the air, and then in an awfully mysterious way, going clear through the window, and disappearing in the air above.

"Guid preserve us a'," said the auld man, rubbing his eyes, "what can be the meaning o' that?"

"It's the deil! It's the deil himsel'," cried the women.

"Haud yer tongues, ye jauds," said the guidman. "Hoo can it be the deil, when he's no cloven-footed? Come oot wi' me, Jamie, and Tam, come you tae, and see if we canna catch the thief."

When they got outside they could see nothing. There was not even a footmark on the soft soil beneath the window.

"It's maist extrornar'," said the guidman, wiping the perspiration from his brow, and catching his breath as if he had been running a mile. "This has been an awfu' nicht; there's first ma dream, and me waukening wi' ma face wat wi' sowans, and next here's something that seems to be neither beast nor body making free wi' ma guids in the pantry."

When they got into the house again, Jock and Rab were coming down the stair, as if they were just awakened, although some of the lassies could

not help remarking that Rab's mouth and chin
looked "unco creeshie like."

They were informed of the doings of the
mysterious visitor, and Jock hazarded the remark
that it was likely to be some hungry, drucken
tinkler.

The lassies held to their belief that it was the
deil or else a brownie. But everybody was
pleased to find that nothing but the food from
the pantry was missing, so they all went back to
their beds again till morning.

*          *          *          *          *

When Rab was sticking fast in the pantry
window, Jock, whose window was just over the
one in the pantry, suspecting what was the matter
with Rab, let down a sheet, and whispered to him
to catch hold. Rab eagerly seized it with his
hands and teeth, dragging himself out of the
window of the pantry, and scrambled in at the
window of the loft.

Neither Jock nor Rab ever said anything on
the subject, although often when they went back
to the guidman's house to court the lassies, the

story of that awfu' nicht and the mysterious
visitor was told and retold, getting every time
more wonderful and mysterious in the telling.

But when Jock had married Jeanie, and Rab
had got Jenny for a wife, Rab told Jenny how he
was the Brownie in the pantry. Jenny only
laughed and told him wherever he was he should
openly eat his fill, and pooch nane.

**PHAROS** the king of the beautiful island of Freyvangar, was blessed with a good queen, and a lovely and dutiful daughter; yet he was very miserable.

In a rocky islet, just opposite his chief city, lived a terrible monster called the Ræsvelgur.* Every night it swam over to King Pharos' land, and to whatever part it came it left the people weeping and wailing; for it seized the goodliest youths, and the fairest maidens in its terrible jaws, and carried them off to its rocky cave.

The islanders who tried to oppose it were crushed under its feet, or mangled to death by its horrible teeth. The king was distracted. At length he sent his heralds all over the world to proclaim that whoever slew the monster should have his beautiful daughter, the Princess Phareyes, for his bride, and be declared heir to the throne of Freyvangar. The fame of the princess's beauty and goodness had spread over the world, so princes and knights came eagerly from all parts to slay the Ræsvelgur.

Now amongst those who came were two princes who, above the rest, were resolved to win the prize. One was Sycomax, king of the dark land of Embla. He was haughty, overbearing.

* Hræsvelgur means literally Raw-swallower.

and cruel to his subjects, and only resolved to slay the monster in order that he might be able to boast that he had the loveliest princess in the world for a bride, and that he was heir to the beautiful island of Freyvangar.

The other was Coralin, prince of the Island of Pearls. He fell madly in love with the princess the first time he saw her; and, content with the rich kingdom full of beautiful gardens, singing fountains, and pearl-built palaces he already possessed, he did not care to inherit Freyvanger, if he could only win the princess. She, for her part, was equally smitten with Coralin, and desired nothing so much as that he might slay the Rasvelgur, and become her husband.

## II.

ONE night all the princes' lords, knights, and men lay in wait for the monster; one party was in ships and the other on the shore. They waited till long past midnight, and as it never came they began to hope or fear that they had scared it away. Some of the party were for moving back to the palace, others for waiting longer.

Prince Coralin, who stood in the front rank of the shore party, suddenly cried out,

" It comes."

Instantly a great stillness came upon the men, and they could hear the sounds made by the distant swimming Ræsvelgur as it buffeted the waves with its half-webbed and clawed feet.

The ships were seen to steal out towards the distant islet, and when they got between the monster and his cave, the glare of their torches shone red on the sea.

As the Ræsvelgur approached them the men on shore could see a black shapeless mass which

kirned * and buffeted the water till it shone like
fire. Nearer and nearer it came; the knights
grasped their swords and spears more firmly,
breathing quickly, as they prepared for the onset.

When the monster came near enough for the
men to see its horrible face, some fell down faint-
ing or in convulsions of terror, and many in the
back ranks fled in dismay.

The resolute ones remained, headed by Coralin
and Sycomax. As the monster's fore feet touched
the strand, Coralin sprang forward and aimed a
blow between its eyes; there was a sharp crack,—
the sword was broken off short by the hilt. With
an earth-shaking roar, the Ræsvelgur advanced to
destroy the unarmed prince. But Sycomax, and
several others who disdained to be behind Coralin
in courage, came driving in with their spears at the
monster's head. The roars of the beast were
terrible. Lashing the water with his tail, he came
tearing in upon the men; spears and swords were
shivered against his sides or broken by the sweep
of his cruel paws. Some of the knights were

* Churned.

overcome by his hot stifling breath or crushed
between his body and the rocks, or crunched and
mangled by his rows of grisly teeth. Shouts,
groans, and curses mingled with the thunders of
the Ræsvelgur, and the noise of the vexed waters,
and the men began to give way.

But Coralin, who had caught up the sword of
a man who had fainted, watched his opportunity,
and by climbing by the horny nobs on the
Ræsvelgur's side, and by digging his dagger
between the scales, he reached the rough saw-like
ridge of the monster's back. Creeping forward to
the neck, he felt about till he found a joint between

the scales; into this he put the point of his sword, then throwing all his weight upon the weapon, he drove it deep down into the monster's flesh.

With a hideous and unearthly shriek, the Ræsvelgur sprang backward into the water. Coralin held on by the sword he had driven so firmly home, and although mauled by being dashed against the jagged points of the Ræsvelgur's back, he never lost his hold. The beast continued to go back rapidly into the water, bellowing hideously and belching forth on the men in front. As soon as his fore-paws reached deep water, he swang his body round and made for his island cave.

Seeing this, the princes and knights shouted to Coralin to leap down. He hesitated an instant, as if about to leap, but suddenly resolving to keep the advantage he had gained, he waved his hand to his comrades, and allowed himself to be carried out to sea on the monster's back.

As the Ræsvelgur passed the ships, he was saluted with a shower of arrows; but one of the vessels venturing too near and being crashed in by one stroke of the monster's tail, those on board the other ships turned their attention to saving the lives of the drowning crew and then the fleet made for the shore.

Sycomax stood with the rest of the chiefs on the cliff above the shore, tracing by its track of phosphoric fire the flight of the Ræsvelgur. He ground his teeth with rage at the thought that Coralin should excel him in coolness and daring. But he comforted himself with the reflection that Coralin would soon either be destroyed by the Ræsvelgur, or would perish of hunger. Yet pride would not let Sycomax abandon the attempt to slay the monster and win the prize: all night long he tossed restlessly on his bed planning how he might gain his end.

### III.

MEANWHILE Coralin held on by the sword hilt and lay quiet on the monster's back. When the beast reached the rocky islet, it crawled wearily up between the rocks to a huge black cave, into which at high tide the water came dashing and roaring As soon as the head of the beast was

within the entrance, Coralin slid down to the
ground and climbing up the steep rocks above
the cave sat down to think what he should do.

He began to fear that he had acted rashly
and fool-hardily; for, even supposing he was able
to deprive the Ræsvelgur of life, how was it
possible for him to escape from the islet when
every ship shunned the dreadful spot? While he
was perishing, Sycomax would be wooing the
Princess, and though he believed in her pre-
ference for himself, Coralin was too well aware
of the unscrupulous character of Sycomax, not to
dread the worst.

At daybreak, on looking down on the rocks
between which the sea swelled and foamed, he
saw a great mass of spars and cordage, the
remains of a wreck cast ashore on the islet.
Hope began to revive as a plan of escape dawned
on his mind. He went down and looked into the
mouth of the cave. Amongst a pile of human
bones he saw the monster lying asleep and
breathing heavily.

Going to the wreck, he half dragged, and half

rolled with infinite labour, the largest piece of
timber he could find, and by exerting his utmost
strength, he managed to place its two ends on the
low rocks on each side of the cave, but some
yards distant from the entrance, so that it would
bar, or seem to bar, the progress of the Ræsvelgur
when, in its nightly excursions, it left the cave.

Coralin saw that the centre of the mast
opposite the cave was well garnished with iron
hooks and bands, so that it could not easily be
bitten through by the monster

To each end of the mast or large spar he tied
a strong rope; the other ends of the ropes he led up
to a ledge of rock above the entrance of the cave.
Having thus completed his preparations, he went
to a safe place and lay down, and though it was
the day time, he was soon fast asleep.

## IV.

On the same morning Sycomax, having likewise formed his plans, took one of his galleys
with thirty picked fighting men, and the same
number of rowers. At the bow of the ship he
placed an anchor, which his great strength en-
abled him to throw to some distance. The day
was spent in preparing and exercising his men
for the renewal of the combat with the Ræsvelgur. When the sun set, he gave the word, and
the galley was rowed out and lay half-way between Freyvangar and the cave of the Ræsvelgur.

Meanwhile, about sunset, Coralin awoke and
took his way to the ledge above the entrance to
the cave. He saw that the mast was in its place
across the passage to the deep water.

The ropes that led from the ends of the mast he took in his hands, and sat patiently waiting for the appearance of the monster.

The tide began to flow into the cave beneath, and soon he heard the loud howling yawns of the awakened Ræsvelgur. Coralin's nerves were strained to their utmost, and his heart beat loudly and violently as he heard the heavy feet of the beast trampling over the bones within the cave.

Soon its huge head was thrust out, as it made straight through the shallow water for the open sea.

When it reached the mast, it seized it with its teeth, and was lifting its fore feet to tear it down, when, like a meteor, Coralin came flying suddenly down upon the monster's back. In an instant he drew the ropes tight and lashed them firmly round the hilt of the sword in the Ræsvelgur's neck. When the monster felt himself thus reined, bitted, and bridled, he tugged at the mast with his claws, but the more he struggled the more painful the wound in his neck became; so, giving up the struggle, he threw himself into deep water, and bellowing hideously, swam in the direction of the island of Freyvangar.

Coralin found that he had the monster in some degree under his control, and that he could guide him by the ropes attached to the mast in his mouth.

Thinking thus to take him alive, he let the

Ræsvelgur swim in the direction of the King's palace without hindrance. But suddenly he saw the torches of the galley gleam on the water, and as the light flashed on the flag that hung at the poop, he knew it was the vessel of Sycomax.

Coralin instantly resolved to slay the monster before his rival approached. But how was this to be done? Examining the ropes, he saw that they were not likely to come loose or let the mast which held the monster's jaws open slip from its place. He crept over the horny forehead between the monsters wild gleaming eyes, and swang himself into the huge cavernous mouth. At first the change from the cool air outside to the hot breath from the monster's throat almost suffocated him; but overcoming his faintness, he crept down into the black stifling throat till he came to a place whose strong pulsations showed the heart lay there. Pointing his long keen dagger to the spot against which the heart beat strongest, he placed his breast against the hilt and drove the blade in with all his force.

The monster gave such a shriek of agony that Coralin for a moment felt pity for this destroyer of thousands; but the hot dark blood spurting out like a flood upon him, soon drove him to think of

his own safety. He passed upward to the top of
the throat, whence he saw the monster's teeth
crunching against the iron-bound mast, and he felt
the whole body rolling wildly about in its dying
agony.

As the last convulsive shiver thrilled through
the monster's body, and it leapt half out of the
water and fell on its side, Coralin lost his footing, and his head striking violently against the
mast, he lay stunned or perhaps dead.

The water came pouring in at the dead monster's mouth, but Coralin's head was kept high and
dry by the mast on which it rested.

## V.

SYCOMAX and his men had not been idle. As
soon as they caught sight of the Ræsvelgur, they
gave way with their oars. The chief stood beside
the anchor ready to fling it when they were near
enough, and the fighting men stood by with their
long barbed spears.

The vessel was rapidly approaching the
monster, when suddenly its awful death-shriek

smote on their ears, and the men started with horror at the sound. To their amazement, they beheld the huge beast writhing, struggling, and lashing the water with its paws and tail, and after leaping half out of the water, falling on its side.

For some time the men were afraid to approach it, but seeing that it was seemingly quite dead, Sycomax ordered the men back to their oars. When they had rowed near enough, he seized the well-tempered anchor and flung it with all his force at the Ræsvelgur. Finding it had caught firmly, he brought the anchor rope round to the stern of the vessel, and bidding his men give way with the oars, they steered back to the city of King Pharos in Freyvangar, towing the huge body behind them.

As they approached the shore nearest the king's palace, day was breaking. Sycomax ordered his trumpeters to sound a triumphal march; this they did so effectually that the greater part of the inhabitants of the city came running down to the shore to meet them. Some hung

back when they caught sight of the huge monster,
but the cheers of the crew reassured them.

The inhabitants were wild with joy when they
found their terrible scourge was dead, and that
they might now sleep in peace.  Nothing was
done that day but feasting, singing, drinking, and
dancing.

When Sycomax landed, all hands were set to
work to bring the dead Ræsvelgur ashore.  By
the help of the receding tide this was soon accomplished.

Kneeling  before  King  Pharos,  Sycomax
claimed, as the slayer of the Ræsvelgur, the hand
of the Princess Phareyes and the heirship of the
Island of Freyvangar.

Pharos was troubled ; he had  no  great liking
for the king of the dark land of Embla, and he
knew, moreover, that his daughter's heart was set
on Coralin.   But  as  he  thought the prince was
surely dead, and as his own word could not be
broken, he drew forward the princess to join her
an ds  to those of Sycomax.

But ere  this was accomplished, a scream of

terror rang out from the crowd who stood beside the dead monster, and the king, the princess, and Sycomax went to see what it meant.

## VI.

IT happened that the king's jester, who was with the others examining the Ræsvelgur, began to amuse the people by approaching the monster's mouth and then jumping back with well-acted terror, making the women and children laugh, though their hearts leapt to their mouths each time he thus startled them.

Suddenly he marched forward, and lifting the hanging upper lip, put his head into the huge cavernous mouth. Hearing what sounded like a groan proceeding from the throat of the beast, and seeing something in a glittering dress lying at the back of its mouth, he staggered back with pale face and shaking limbs, screaming and howling in genuine terror. The women and children screamed for sympathy, and everybody believed something dreadful had happened. Some of Coralin's men who stood by rushed forward, and prising open the enormous jaws, kept them asunder with their spears.

Prince Coralin, who was just recovering his senses, raised himself and sat looking dreamily at them. And just as King Pharos, his daughter, and his would-be son-in-law arrived on the spot, Coralin came staggering forward from the monster's throat. The people gave a cry of astonishment, which was immediately changed to a shout of joy as the princess, with a cry of delight, recognised, and ran forward to meet her lover, whom she had thought devoured by the Ræsvelgur or swallowed by the sea.

But the king of the dark land of Embla, who began to fear that he might lose the princess and her dowry after all, rushed between them, and catching up the princess suddenly in his arms, dashed down in the direction of his own vessel.

The princess gave a great cry of "Coralin! Coralin! to my aid, my Coralin!"

He stared for a moment as if he had been too suddenly awakened from sleep; then a terrible look came into his eyes, and he sprang forward and caught his rival by the throat. Sycomax set down the princess and grappled with his adversary, who, weak from want of food, newly recovered from his swoon, and quite unarmed, had little chance against the dark king. Nevertheless, he clung manfully to his rival's throat, till they fell together. Sycomax rolled over till he got the prince beneath him; then, planting his knee on his chest, he drew his dagger from its sheath, and raised it to plunge it into Coralin's heart. As the dagger was descending, Sycomax received a stroke from the cudgel of the jester, which laid him senseless, while the dagger was buried harmlessly in the sand.

The rest of the people, who had been struck powerless by the suddenness with which all this had taken place, now came crowding round.

The beautiful princess, heedless of everything but Coralin, caught his pale face between her fair hands and kissed him on the lips.

This seemed to revive him in a wonderful manner, and he immediately rose. The jester produced a flask of rare liquor, without which he never went abroad, and placed it to Coralin's mouth. Soon the colour came into his cheeks, and he told the princess and the people to look whose sword it was that had pierced the monster's neck, and desired the king to send his own men into the Ræsvelgur's throat, and see whose dagger had given the monster his death-wound.

When these were brought, the people saw that Coralin was truly the slayer of the Ræsvelgur. The prince told them how he had achieved its death, and Sycomax's men confessed that the monster was dead before they had reached it, and that they had done nothing but towed it ashore.

Sycomax, who was now coming to his senses, was placed on board his own galley, King Pharos and Coralin sending with him rich presents, for they were all aware that in towing the dead monster to land, the dark king had unwittingly saved the prince's life. Sycomax was appeased by the value of the gifts, and setting sail for his own dark land, troubled the island of Freyvangar no more.

Prince Coralin wedded Princess Phareyes and carried her to his home in the Island of Pearls, where, loving each other truly to the end, they lived happily all the rest of their days.

## THE TRIAL OF THE SUITORS.

THERE was once a well-tochered farmer's daughter who was very beautiful, and as clever as she was bonny. She had many admirers. But two of her sweethearts distanced all the rest, and the lass was undecided which of the two to choose.

One, when he came awooing, was plainly dressed, and quiet and modest in his demeanour. He got leave to stay in the kitchen. The other

came dressed like a lord ; he was loud and bragging in his conversation, and was always accompanied by his man-servant. This suitor was taken
into the parlour, and he was the one the girl's
mother urged her to marry, although the lass
herself liked the other one best.

Before accepting any of them for her husband
the girl resolved to test what each of them was
like when at home. So she disguised herself like
a poor old woman, and went to the modest suitor's
house and asked for a night's lodging.

The mother of the modest suitor received her
in a kindly way, and made her
welcome to sit beside herself,
and chat by the fire till her son
would come home.

When the son came home,
the lass slipped into a corner
more in the shadow, and drew
her cloak well about her face.

" Who have you here ? " said the son.

" Only a poor old woman that I have promised
a night's lodging," said the mother.

"That's right!" said the son; "see and make her as comfortable as you can."

The mother spread the supper-table and bade the poor woman draw in. But the lass desired to be excused, and said, if they would allow her, she would take a bit on her knee where she was, for she was afraid her sweetheart might recognise her if she sat at the table.

The mother gave her a liberal supply on a plate, and the son went over once or twice and gave her some specially nice bits.

Then the son went out to look at his horses, and as the lass said she was tired, the mother took the opportunity of putting her into the kitchen bed, opposite the fire.

When the son came in again, he asked his mother if she had given the poor old woman plenty of bed-clothes. The mother said she thought she had. But the son said, "Old folk are aye cold," and took some more blankets and happed the old woman up.

Then she heard him say to his mother as he went off to his own bed, "See that the poor body has a good breakfast after I am gone away. For I shall be off early, and she will likely be tired and lie long.

The lass said to herself,

" He is a kind good man, and I like him the best, although my mother wants me to take the dandy." Then she fell asleep.

Awaking next morning, the mother set a plentiful breakfast before her, and urged her to eat heartily, as she was travelling and had a long day before her. When she was going, she put into her hands some food wrapped up for her to eat by the way. The girl thanked her sincerely, and taking her way home, got there all safe without anybody being a bit the wiser.

That evening the modest suitor came to see the lass, and she was even kinder than usual to him, yet she would give him no definite promise till she saw how she fared at the house of the one who came so gallantly attired and attended.

Next night, disguised as before, she set off as a poor old woman to visit the house of the gay dashing sweetheart. He was not at home when

I

she arrived, but his mother opened the door. The lass begged for a night's lodgings. The mother said she dared not let her come in, for her son would be angry if he knew her harbour any poor people. The girl said she was tired and could go no farther, and implored the mother to let her lie in a corner of the kitchen till morning.

"As you are a clean-looking body, I will risk it for once," said the mother; "but mind, I can give you nothing to eat, and you must lie quiet on some straw in a dark corner."

The lass professed to be glad of any kind of shelter. She was admitted into the kitchen, and lay down in a dark corner, while the mother worked at a table.

After a while the dashing suitor came home, and the lass was surprised to hear how harsh and grating his voice sounded, as in a surly manner he demanded his supper.

" What will you have?" said the mother ; " beef, or bread and cheese?"

" Great powers !" said the dashing sweetheart, "do you wish to ruin me? You know how I have to keep up appearances, and is my money to be fooled away on such extravagances as beef suppers, when I have so much to pay for my clothes ?"

" Well," said the mother, "the cauld kail that was left from your dinner the day before yester-day is in the aumrie."

" Ay, that's something like ; bring it."

When the kail was brought there was a lot of dead mice floating in it, for the dashing suitor would not permit his mother to keep a cat on account of the expense.

But he set to work, and began supping the cauld kail. Each time he took up a mouse he drew it carefully through his teeth so as to lose none of the kail, and so he got on with his supper.

Afterwards, when he had supped his fill, and

was resting, he caught sight of somebody lying in
the corner.

He started up and said to his mother sharply,
" Who is that ? "

"Oh!" said his mother, " it is just a poor
woman that was not able to go any farther, and I
let her lie down."

"A pretty story!" said the son.   "Off she goes
at once.   A fine thing for me to be eaten out of
house and home by a parcel of lazy beggars.   Put
her out, I say."

The mother begged him to control himself,
and told him that it was not an ordinary beggar
but a poor old woman who was neat and clean
that she had not given her a bite of anything
since she entered, and she would go without
supper herself if he would let the woman
remain.

"She  may remain then, on that condition,"
said the son, who was a miser at heart, and
grudged every bite his mother ate.

In the morning, when the lass was going
away, the mother told her she was sorry that she

could give her nothing fit to eat. For her son kept everything locked up, and only gave her a very scanty allowance, but rather than the lass should absolutely starve the mother had managed to secrete a crust of bread from her own breakfast, and this she pressed into the lassie's hand as she went away.

The lass got home without any one knowing where she had been.

In the evening the dashing gallant, attended by his man, came to see her. He inquired after her health in a tender insinuating way, which the lady had once thought to be an index to his fine, affable, and kindly disposition, but she thought on his harsh tones when he spoke to his mother, and knew that he was only acting a part to deceive her.

Her mother led the fine suitor as usual into the parlour, and bade her daughter go in and entertain him. But the lass would not go, and continued to sit in the kitchen at her spinning-wheel.

Seeing that the lass would not come ben the

house, the dashing suitor came with his man into the kitchen, and leant up against the chimney, to talk to the fair lass.

After a good deal of bragging conversation, a great part of which was carried on between the suitor and his man for the lassie's benefit, the gallant said, " I am afraid I have dined too well to-day," and he opened his mouth and gave a great windy belch.

" What makes you rift so, master ? " said the servant.

" Apple pies and old ale," said the gallant.

The lass could stand his deceit and pretension no longer, so she said, " I think you mistake ; it was not

> ' Apple pies and old ale,'
> But dioon'd mice in cauld kail."

The gallant tried for a moment to brazen it out, but he could not look the lass in the face, so seizing his hat he went off in a hurry, followed by his astonished servant, and never again came acourting there.

The lass married the modest suitor. She had no cause to repent her bargain, for he was as good as he seemed to be, and they lived content and happily all their days.

## I.

ONILD was the only son of Seigrid, Jarl of Vasader. His father, the Jarl, dying when Yonild was about eighteen years old, his mother

Donhilda, a few months afterwards, married a strong, rough viking, named Thiblun, who had been a bold warrior in his day.

But when Thiblun became master in the halls of Donhilda, he filled the castle with his rough companions, and passed the time in drinking and rioting. When Donhilda tried to remonstrate with him  in one of his drunken fits, he thrust her from him with such force that she fell on the stone floor. Yonild, who stood by, sprang at Thiblun's throat, and held a grip in spite of blows, till his step-father began to grow black in the face; then some of the wild companions came to the rescue, and tearing Yonild from the half-suffocated Thiblun, bore him from the hall and thrust him out.

When Thiblun came to himself, he was mad with passion, and swore by Hela and all the ghosts of Niflheim, to slay Yonild at the first opportunity. Yonild returned to the hall that night at supper-time. As soon as he came in at the door, Thiblun, without a word, threw his great dagger with all his might at Yonild's head. The weapon grazed his cheek, and buried itself nearly to the hilt in the oaken door. Thiblun then snatched up his sword, and springing from the dais, rushed down the hall to slay his step-son. But the shrieks of Donhilda and the women caused the men to lay hold on Thiblun, and force him back to his place. His mother then half dragged, half led Yonild out of the hall, down the stairs, and out past the spence, and implored him to fly till Thiblun's rage was overpast.

Yonild was fearless for himself, but when his mother begged that he would go for her sake, he could not refuse her. So he left her and went out into the darkness, while Donhilda and the women sobbed at the gate.

## II.

YONILD lay that night in a glen close by the castle, and early next morning turned his back on his father's lands, and set out to find such fortune as the heavens might send him.

By noon he had travelled many a mile, and came near a town which lay low on the northern

shores of a wide firth.   He was glad to see
houses once more, so that he might buy something to eat; for though he had plucked berries
by the way, he missed the more substantial food
he had been accustomed to in his father's house.

When he got to the middle of the long street
where the runic cross stood, he saw a crowd of
boys pelting some one who lay at the foot of the
cross, while the men and women of the place
stood by laughing and encouraging the boys.

Making his way through the crowd, he saw
it was a poor-looking, bent, old, and decrepit
woman that the boys were pelting with clay.
Tears streamed from her eyes, and mixed with
the clay that stuck to her face.

Yonild ran to the place where she lay, and
stood between her and the boys; then turning on
them with flashing eyes and knitted brows, he
said,

" Think shame of yourselves, to treat a poor
old helpless woman like that."

" She a witch ! she a witch !" cried the boys.

" She has an evil eye, and traffics with the

fiend. Take care of yourself, young master,"
cried the men and women.

"I'll risk that," said Yonild; "call in your boys;
begone, you little cowards."

The men and women sauntered away, and the
boys slunk back.

Yonild raised the old woman, and bidding her
lean on him, the pair crossed the open space and
went up the hill path that led to the old woman's
dwelling.

It was a poor enough place, but neat and
clean. When the woman had washed the clay
and dirt from her face, Yonild saw that she was
younger and stronger than he had at first
thought.

She set meat before him plentifully, and when
he had eaten his fill, she said, "Are you not afraid
to eat and drink in a witch's chamber?"

Yonild replied smilingly,

"Do you think I trust those foolish boys and
ignorant fishermen? Besides, even a witch would
scarcely injure one who tried to do her a good
turn."

She fell on her knees before him, and like a
dog licked and kissed his hands.

" May the bonny brave red-bearded Thor bless
you for your trust in me.   No, no, I will never
harm you, though I am Thrudur the witch, and
worship the old red gods of my fathers instead
of the white Jew God to whom they raise the
carven crosses.   But surely even the white Christ
if he is as good as they say he is, would not be

angry with an old woman for clinging and holding to the gods of her youth, when all the world has turned against them, and their worshippers are hunted and harried by the slaves of the black-robed psalm-singing monks who curse us from the altar. Ay, ay, it is changed days now. The all-wise Odin, the strong and brave Thor, and the gracious Frey are no longer called gods but devils. They were kind to me in their fair days, and I will not be so mean as desert them in the bloody twilight that has enwrapped them. And I have my reward, for Thor grants his gifts as freely now as he did in the old days. Through his power I will give you smooth winds and teach you to sail through the air when the full moon shines on the sea."

Yonild, who thought her crazed, said, "Can Thor give you such power, and yet be powerless to assist you against a troop of boys?"

"Thor did assist me when I asked him, and sent you to my aid."

Yonild did not know what to say to this interpretation of his coming to her assistance, so he held his peace.

She continued, " Now tell me who you are and whence you come ; for surely you are a prince's son of the old race ; I know the falcon eyes and Jarl fair hair."

Yonild told her what had lately taken place in his father's house, and how he feared for his mother.

"Fear not for her," said Thrudur.   "This very night I'll weave the spell of Iduna, the keeper of the golden apples, about your house, and your mother shall live in peace and safety.   And for your own reward, I can teach you how you may gain the helmet of Asgard, which no sword can pierce, and which will make you walk invisible when you choose.   Then you shall have the sandals of Hermod, by which you shall fly in safety over perilous seas."                          ·

Although Yonild regarded these words as nothing but the vain babble of a half-crazed old woman, he could not prevent his eyes sparkling with delight at the mere thought of possessing such wondrous things.

" I   can   read   your   face,"   said   Thrudur.

"You think I am bragging in madness. See here!"

She pulled aside a curtain at the back of the apartment, disclosing an arched doorway in the rock of the hill, against whose side the house was built; then she said,

" Now enter and tell me what you see."

Yonild entered what seemed a large dimly but naturally lighted cave, and cried back,

" I see a circle of tall stones; there is an altar plated with iron, and on it stands a vase of brass smeared with blood. A great silver ring hangs by a chain from the rocky roof, and a sword is passed through the ring."

" Bring me that; it is the sword Fail-me never," said Thrudur. Yonild stepped across to the centre of the cave, and taking the sword from the silver ring, brought it back with him to the outer apartment.

" Now pull it from its sheath."

Yonild drew Fail-me-never out, and a dazzling light filled the place. The blade, which was engraved with forgotten runes, shone like a diamond.

K

"Take it to the door-stone and see how it cuts," said the witch. Yonild went and struck the huge stone which was placed outside the door. The sword went through the hard granite as if it had been water instead of stone.

"It is a rare sword," said Yonild, handing it back to Thrudur.

"Keep it," said she ; "it is the only gift I have to give you, though I can teach you to win rarer things, if you have the mind."

No longer doubting her power, Yonild expressed his joy at his good fortune in winning her favour, and his desire to win the helmet of Asgard and the flying shoes of Hermod. "But," he added, "I fear you will think me a greedy robber if I thus readily accept of those treasures, for what will be left for other friends if you lavish on me all that your power procures ?"

"Fear not for that ; besides the gifts are Thor's, not mine ; nor shall you win them if you are unworthy. Brave Ving Thor will surely see to that. But since you have agreed to try the quest,

leave me till moonrise; I have spells to set awork-
ing for your aid.

## III.

PROMISING to return with the rising of the moon,
Yonild left the witch's cottage on the hill and
strolled down towards the shores of the firth.
But avoiding the town, he reached the shore at a
point where stood an old grey ruined castle, bleak,
hoary, and scarred by fire.

He lay down on the rock at its base, and with
his eyes on the heaving, seething, fresh, clear,
restless and resistless water, he let his mind weave
the web of his future fortune. For he was already
filled with visions of what he would do when he
had gained the wondrous helmet and the flying
sandals. He would explore the world and its
famous cities. He would walk unseen in kings'
palaces and visit the hidden treasures, or the enchanting gardens, where the fair princesses he had
heard of passed their days in growing as sweet
and lovely as the flowers which bloomed around

them.   He would fly to the moon, and sit and
hear the sprites singing those melodious songs
which only at rare intervals reach the earthly
poet's ear.

He was glad—wildly, impatiently, and restlessly glad.   He started up and sprang from rock
to rock as he followed the windings of the shore.

The sun set behind the hills, and as the arc of
faint light which heralded the coming of the moon
rose over the east he turned and took his way up
the face of the hill to Thrudur's dwelling.   Before
he reached the door the full orb of the moon had
soared above the surface of the water and made a
stream of glittering, shifting, heaving silver from
shore to horizon.   It looked a fit pathway for
the golden chariots of the gods to roll from
heaven to earth.

He entered the cottage.

All was dark.   Thrudur was gone.   A chill
went to his heart.   This, then, was the end of the
dreams which had been raised in his mind by
the wild ravings of the crazy witch-woman.   He
might have known better than build on a founda-

tion so feeble. But he had builded, and the falling of his airy castles filled his heart for the moment with a stour of exceeding bitterness.

Suddenly he thought of the cavern. Thrudur might be there. So, drawing the curtain, he knocked loudly at the door, and cried,

" Thrudur, are you there ?"

"Yes, I am here. Enter," said Thrudur, opening the door.

Yonild went in, and Thrudur bolted and barred the door behind him.

The place was only dimly and mistily lighted by some glimmering and distorted rays of the moon which straggled in through an opening in the centre of the cavern. The huge stones stood weird, ghost-like, and cold in the feeble light. A spark or point of fire appeared over the altar on which lay some animal, tied and ready for the slaughter.

Ranged in a circle on the middle of the floor of the cave were six objects, which at first he took for huge boulders, but on placing his hand on one, he found it was a living being. On looking more

narrowly he perceived that what he took for
stones were six crouching women. They were
muttering and praying ecstatically, and took no
notice of Yonild as he passed them.

Thrudur led Yonild up to the altar and bade
him kneel. When he had done so, she drew a
sharp knife from her girdle and plunged it into
the animal that lay on the altar. As she did so,
she said in a loud voice,

" I devote thee to Odin."

She then took a brush, and dipping it in the
blood of the victim, sprinkled it first upon her
own face, then upon Yonild, and afterwards on
each of the kneeling women.

Then she led Yonild into the centre of the
ring of praying women, and he knelt with his
face to the altar. Thrudur took her place in
the circle, and crouched with the other women
around him.

Their prayers and mutterings became louder,
more earnest and imploring ; they all spoke at one
time, although no two said exactly the same words
together.

" Oh, Thou, all-Father," they cried,
" Hear us, great Odin,
  We beseech and conjure thee,
  Give success to our work,
  Sun, Ruler, and Father.


" List to us, Thor,
  Rock-Splitter, Storm-Ruler ;
  We implore thee to hear us,
  Come to us, Red-Beard,
  Who smitest the nations.


" Beautiful Frey,
  Who givest the sunshine,
  Smile on our spells
  And fire us with ardour ;
  So shall we conquer."


Then their words were lost to Yonild, for they began to chaunt fast and furiously in an unknown tongue, bowing their faces to the floor and gradually creeping inward till all their hands rested on the head of Yonild.

Though his brain began to feel on fire, and his flesh quivered as he felt their rough, gnarled, but not unkindly fingers on his body, his mind never flinched, and he kept his eyes on the altar.

" All tongues are alike to Odin, the all-Father." cried Thrudur."

" We are seven who have served thee, Thor, when the strong men were slain and the weak ones forsook thee," cried the second of the women.

" Frey, we have loved thee and faithfully served thee in sunshine and shadow," said the third.

" Thor, Thor is coming, I feel his warm breath that precedes the thunder," said the fourth.

" List how the winds sough o'er the cavern ! they are the heralds that tell of his coming," said the fifth.

" Look where his lightnings play over the cloudlands !" said the sixth.

" Hear how his thunders roll o'er the islands." cried the seventh.

" He comes ! the brave Thor who never forsakes us, comes !" cried all the women together.

There had been a sound of a light wind, which

gradually but rapidly increased till it became the roll of distant thunder. Lightnings played about the roof of the cavern and flickered over the altar. The thunder became louder, and as the witches screamed together in ecstasy, " He comes, the brave Thor !" a blaze of fire filled the cavern, followed by an ear-splitting crash of thunder ; the rocks opened, giving a glimpse of the outside sky, and a mailed figure, lighted up by electric fire, stood upon the altar.

The witches gave a shout of joy and cried, " Glory to our mighty Thor, who never forsakes his servants!"

" Speak !" said the figure, in a voice of rolling melodious thunder, " and thrice will I answer."

" Shall he who kneels before thee gain the gifts he covets?" cried the women.

" He shall through Fire," said the figure.

" Shall he who kneels before thee succeed in his desires?" cried the women.

" He shall by Hope and Labour."

" Shall he who kneels before thee defeat his enemies?" cried the women.

"He shall triumph through Justice. Farewell. Hark! I am called hence."

The women hushed themselves, and a cry, faint as from an immeasurable distance, sighed through the cavern.

"Come to our aid, Thor," cried the faint far-away voices.

"I come!" cried Thor, in answer to the voices.

"Stay!" cried the witches; "grant us your blessing, brave kind Thor.

"'Tis yours always," said the figure, stretching out his hands. Then he darted in flame through the rocks, which closed up again with thundrous crash.

The witches slowly rose, seemingly much exhausted by their prayers and passionate ecstasy.

Thrudur poured out some colourless drink from a flagon, and bade Yonild quaff it. He drank it at once, and the blood coursed with renewed vigour through his veins. Then, in turn, all the women drank of the liquor; first, however, each poured a little on the floor, at the same time saying,

"To the good luck of our God Thor, and of our new guest."

After they had rested for some time, Thrudur whispered to the other women, who nodded and whispered back to her; then she came to Yonild and said,

"You must go now, and leave us here, but stay this night in my cottage; to-morrow you shall learn what it is you must do. We fly this night to Vasader to work around your father's house the spells that will bring peace and happiness to your mother."

Yonild passed out of the cavern into the cottage, and wrapping himself up in some skins he found there, soon fell asleep.


## IV.

In the morning he was awakened by Thrudur, who had prepared a breakfast for him. He arose, scarce remembering at first where he was, but as the events of the night before came to his mind, he knew not what to think of them. He gazed

curiously at his strange hostess, and waited for
her to speak. She did not say a word, however,
till he had done eating. Then she poured out
some of the colourless liquor he had tasted the
night before, and bade him drink, telling him that
he had need of it, for he had rare work before
him that day.

Yonild took a fair draught, and felt his hopes
and spirit rise when he had done so.

"Listen carefully to me," said Thrudur, "for I
can but spare you few words, for I am tired with
my sail through last night's moonlight to your
father's house. Your mother now dwells in peace,
and you must fulfil the destiny which Thor has
sanctioned. Take up Fail-me-never, the sword I
gave you yesterday, and set out without fear.
Keep by the shore till you reach a glen, by which
a stream flows into the sea. Follow that stream
till you come to two lakes; take the road that lies
between them, and you shall find the magic
helmet of Asgard and the flying shoes of Hermod.
I cannot tell you more, save that when once upon
that road you must not turn, even for fire or

flames, or any other terror, till you have obtained the gifts of Thor. Farewell; I am a weary;" and she staggered to a seat.

Yonild saw that she was weak and suffering, and he implored her to let him stay with her till she was better.

"Rest, rest is all I want," she said; "you must not stay, but push forward while the power of my spells is strong. Again I bid you farewell."

Seeing it useless to say more, Yonild thanked her earnestly for her great kindness to him, and went out of the cottage.

He soon reached the shore, and following Thrudur's directions, came in due time to the road between the two lakes.

The sea was far behind him, wild rocky hills girdled the lakes, and came curving in to meet the road, so that far away in front they entirely closed in, and arched over his pathway. The spot was lonely, not even a beast or a bird was to be seen.

He sat down and rested for a little, and ate of

the food Thrudur had put into his scrip. He felt a
mysterious desire to delay entering the lonely and
unknown pathway before him. It was not fear
he felt, but a reluctance to commit himself to an
irrevocable destiny. Soon, however, overcoming
the idle thoughts that counselled delay, he started
up and entered the pathway. As he proceeded
the light gradually grew fainter, not because day
was declining, but owing to the rocks on each side
of and above him getting closer, and closer, to the
path ; and for the last few miles they had entirely

excluded the direct light of day, and came down
to meet the earth in front, as well as on his right
hand and on his left, so that he was hemmed in

on three sides by rocks which seemed to defy him to penetrate farther.

But as he left the daylight behind him, and approached the masses of roof-rock which came down to the earth in front, and appeared to be the limit of his road, he perceived a wavering uncertain light coming from a hole in the rocks before him. There lay his path, he knew, and his heart beat quicker as he looked around him on the grim, lonely, overhanging rocks, like huge teeth, ready to crush him on every side, and saw before him a cave of fire.

He clambered up to the opening whence the light proceeded, and crept into the low and narrow passage in which the light became gradually stronger. He heard confused noises, and mocking laughter above, below, and all around him. He felt that he was drawing towards the climax of his adventure, and his heart grew bolder at the thought. Still he crept on, till at last the narrow passage ended in a spacious lofty cave in the centre of which was a mighty ring of hot, high, fierce, and roaring flame, around which stood and sat a row of swarthy dwarfs hammering at anvils, and pulling red-hot bars of metal from the flames.

When Yonild advanced with dazzled eyes from the narrow path, the dwarfs set up a shout of derision.

" Ho, ho !" they cried, " here comes one of the white peacemakers !"

" Yes," cried another, " a fine example of the fine peacemakers who would burn, slay, and destroy everybody who does not think as they do."

" It would be well to teach this youngster that fire is hot and flames burn," said another.

" Ha, ha !" cried the rest, " a nice little jest;" and they rushed forward to seize Yonild.

Yonild quickly drew Fail-me-never from its scabbard, and the blade shone so brightly that the flaming wall of fire paled before it.

" Ah !" cried the dwarfs, drawing back, " that is no earthly weapon. Who are you who venture so boldly into the halls of Muspellheim?"

" I am Yonild, and from great Ving Thor I come."

At the dreaded name of Thor the dwarfs fell on their knees before Yonild, crying,

" What does Ving Thor desire ? Speak ; we will serve thee."

" I conjure you by the name of Thor to tell how I may win the helmet of Asgard and the flying sandals of Hermod," said Yonild.

" We dare not ! we dare not !" cried the dwarfs. " Sutur, our king, would slay us if we rendered up the fairy gifts of Asgard without his knowledge. But you shall ask him for yourself. Come."

Yonild followed them round to the other side of the circle of fire, and through a grim-toothed archway into another and larger cavern, set about with golden pillars, and studded all over with precious stones and all the rare things which men dig from the bosom of the earth.

On a throne of incomparable richness sat the king of the dwarfs, black-browed, swarthy-skinned, sinewy-armed, and eagle-eyed.

The dwarfs, who had accompanied Yonild to the entrance of the hall, fell back at the sight of their king, and returning to the fire-cave, left

I.

Yonild standing alone before Sutur, the Prince of
Muspellheim, the home of elemental fire.

"Whence come you, bold mortal?" said the
king.

"From Thrudur, called the witch, with the
favour and consent of Thor."

"What is your errand?"

"To find the helmet of Asgard and the shoes
of Hermod."

"By my mother Ertha!" said the king, "you
are not blate.* Yet, if you bear a true token
from brave Thor, you shall not lack my help."

"I have no token, if this sword be not one,"
said Yonild, handing the glittering blade to the
king.

Sutur scanned the runes with which it was
graven, and  said, as he handed it back, "It is
enough.   It is a true token, and wrought by my
own knaves.   What, ho! Logi, Modi, and Hrym,
appear!"

Three figures entered, and Sutur, pointing to
Yonild, said,

* Bashful.

"He is our friend, and must pass through the fire. Prepare him truly."

Logi breathed upon Yonild, and his flesh became strong and hard as iron.

Modi approached, and placed his hand on Yonild's heart, and his soul was filled with resistless courage.

Hrym embraced him, and he became proof against flame.

"'Tis enough," said the king. "Lead him to the flaming ring. Farewell."

The three figures led him back to the cave of fire, and told him he must dash bravely through the flames if he would gain the gifts of Asgard.

Yonild drew a deep breath and dashed into the flaming billow. The breath in his throat was fire, and though his body hissed as the hot flames curled round his head and clung fiercely to his limbs, not a hair was singed. So he struggled on with closed eyes; on till the ground beneath his feet gave way, and he felt himself falling into the flaming gulf which was the birthplace of that ring of fire.

Still he fell; he felt the flames grow weaker; they were left above him; still he fell, till at last he felt himself plunging into a lake of deliciously cool water.

He opened his eyes, and what a sight he saw! Rocky caverns and flaming fires had vanished, and he floated on a lake of ravishing beauty, beneath a soft warm sky.  Before him lay an island with marble temples covered by gilded roofs, with shining towers peeping out from amidst groves of cedar and avenues of oak and ash.

Yonild swam to the side of the lake, and mounting the steps that led from the water, saw three figures seated beside a fountain where two swans were floating.

The three who sat by the fountain were singing songs as they wove with unceasing and unresting hands.  It was the Nornir, the awful sisters, who sat beneath a rainbow on the Doom-stead and passed the woollen, silken, and golden threads from hand to hand to make the wondrous web of life.  Verdandi sat in the centre, and her face was sometimes beautifully fair, but ever and anon a cloud passed over her eyes.   The face of

Urd was calm, fair, and serene,
unchanging with the strength
of knowledge and wise power.
But only dimly could he trace the face of Skuld,
for e'en from Yonild, as from every other, was the
Future veiled.   Nor knew he whence she drew her
golden threads which Verdandi snatched from her,

and tossed, sometimes with eager and whiles with careless hands, while Urda, with her ceaseless careful toil, smoothed and spread and wove the threads, and rolled them round her roller of forgotten things.*

The songs of Urd were wise and true. Verdandi's songs were true but fickle, sometimes foolish, sometimes wise. The songs of Skuld were sometimes true, but oftener false; but her sweetest song was the Song of Youth and Hope, and that was the song she was singing when Yonild stood by.

Urda had only her roller; behind the head of Verdandi hung the helmet of Asgard, and at the feet of Skulda the sandals of Hermod lay. Yet Yonild felt he durst not approach the wondrous three, unless at their desire.

The fountain danced and glittered in the light, and sung with the great sisters in all their songs; the swans swam round the fountain in peace and calm till they caught sight of Yonild, when they raised a cry.

* Urd, Verdandi, and Skuld.   The Past, Present, and Future.

The Nornir raised their heads and beckoned Yonild to come forward.

" The gifts you seek are here," cried Verdandi ; "come hither and take them."

He came first to Urda, and she said,

" My gifts are all gone, but look on my face and on my roller of forgotten things, and be thou Wise."

He went next to Verdandi, and she placed the helmet of Asgard on his head, saying as she did so, " Be thou True."

Skulda signed to him to take the sandals ; so he bound the shoes of Hermod to his feet, and tied them round his ankles. Then Skulda said from beneath her veil, " Be thou Brave."

The three waved their hands to him in token of farewell. Yonild flew swiftly up over the temples, towers, and trees, over the shimmering tremulous rainbow, and into the outer atmosphere that girdles all the earth.

## V.

FILLED with joy at his entire success, and borne

up by the sandals of Hermod, Yonild floated on
over cities and palaces, hills and valleys, islands
and firths.

Far away beside the setting sun he saw a land
of purple and pale crimson islands set in a shining sea of golden green. They seemed to be the
Islands of the Blessed, the earthly paradise, of
which he had heard so often, so, rejoicing in his
strength and swiftness, he flew onwards and
onwards to the setting sun.

The sun disappeared, the colour faded out of
the purple islands, and the sea of sheeny green
became darker and darker. Far below him lay
the seas which rolled without a break far as his
eye could reach ; only in those now dark islands of
the west was a place for his tiring feet to be found,
so still onward he flew. But as he approached
nearer to them, a stound of pain smote his heart
when he perceived that they were no islands but
only thick clouds.

For a moment his heart failed when he saw
nothing around him but sea cinctured only by
clouds, and nowhere a speck of land. But

onwards, onwards, was now his only hope of rest. Darkness gathered thick around. The moon rose behind him but was speedily wrapped in clouds, and gave no cheering light. Faint for want of food, and tired with his long flight, it seemed as if every moment he must give up the struggle and drop into the sea.

At last a feeble light rises over the sea before him; is it a star? No, it gradually gets larger as he approaches, and becomes many lights; they are the lamps of a great city in the land of Atlantis.

## VI.

YONILD descended towards the nearest light, and alighted in a garden surrounded by high walls. The light came from the window of a house close by. Looking in, he saw a lady, richly apparelled, in loud, eager, and earnest converse with a cunning-looking old hag.

"Ionis must die, Fanga," said the lady.

"She shall speedily, if you wish it, my queen," said the hag, who seemed to be hard of hearing.

" I do not wish her a speedy death. Let her
suffer the pangs of seeing that her skin is wither-
ing and her flesh rotting. Let her feel that her
fickle adorers, who to-day treat her as if she was
the goddess of beauty, Freyja herself, avoid her
as they would a loathsome pestilence. Do this,
and your reward shall be a royal one."

" Liberal have you always been to me, my
queen," whined Fanga.

" And hark you," said the queen, rising to go,
" let me have more of the water of beauty that
you boasted should aid me to bring back Garngousk to my feet ; and let it be stronger than the
last, for that was powerless."

" The water was truly and well distilled, but
I fear you used it when the stars were on Ionis
side, and unfavourable to you."

" Unfavourable, truly," said the queen ; " for
instead of being, as you promised, again my
devoted slave, Garngousk laughs openly at my
charms, and mocks me to my face, to show the
princess that he only cares for her."

" Your husband's daughter, the princess Ionis, cares not for Garngousk, as I think."

" It seems so, but her indifference only whets his fiery soul the more. I could tear her baby-looking eyes out, when I see her calmly scorn the tender looks of Garngousk, which I, a queen, would give the world, my life, ay, and my soul, to gain."

" Well, well," said the hag, soothingly, "the tender glances and sweeter kisses shall all be yours. My charms have done greater and rarer things."

" The Fates or Furies grant it!"

" The king, your husband, how does he ? "

" My husband! my clod ! my nightmare ! my gentle lump of ice ! Oh, why did I, whose fiery passions rage like a devouring furnace, wed that kind, old, feeble fool ?"

" The king, your husband, is accounted wise, and his first wife's daughter, Ionis, whom you hate, inherits ; so they say"——

" Name her not," said the queen, "except to curse her and her saintly airs of wisdom, and her

doll-like beauty, which have robbed me of the
man who was my dog, my slave, my puppet.   He
said he lived but in my beauty's light; I was his
angel and his loadstar; I laughed his words to
scorn, for then I set but little value on his love or
him.   He left me and began to worship the dawning beauty in Ionis' face.   Now I would give
good name and more than life to win back the
fiery soul whose passion I despised."

"'Tis the way of the world.   But trust me, he
shall again be all he was to you, ay, and more,"
said the hag meaningly.   "Trust but in me;
to-morrow night shall place into your hands
your source of joy with Garngousk, and a sweet
and long revenge on Ionis."

"Till then, farewell; meantime take this
purse as erles,"* said the queen.   Then muffling
herself up in her mantle, she swiftly left the
room.

She passed quite close to Yonild, but seemingly she saw him not, and he knew that the
helmet of Asgard had rendered him invisible.

* Earnest.

He glided into the house noiselessly, and stood by the old witch while she spread for herself a sumptuous supper.

"A brave, weak-headed, passionate lady is our queen Libya," she muttered. "But she is open-handed, and deserves to be well served. She shall be! here's to her health."

She poured out some wine into a cup and drank it, then she filled the cup again and went on with her supper.

Yonild, hungry and thirsty, stood beside the hag, and ate from the table, and drank up the wine she had poured out, and made a good supper.

The hag reached out her hand to the wine cup, and found it empty.

"I could have sworn I filled it; but there's plenty more, and I may take my fill at my ease to-night. To-morrow will be early enough to set to work on the potions. I have everything ready. It is not for nothing that I tell fair fortunes and gallant husbands to the queen's maids; they tell me as rare things in return."

Seeing that the witch had resolved to make herself comfortable and take her ease for the present, Yonild went into another apartment, but afraid that this might be the witch's own chamber, and that he might be discovered as he slept, he went out to the barn. Throwing himself on the straw, he was soon fast asleep.

## VII.

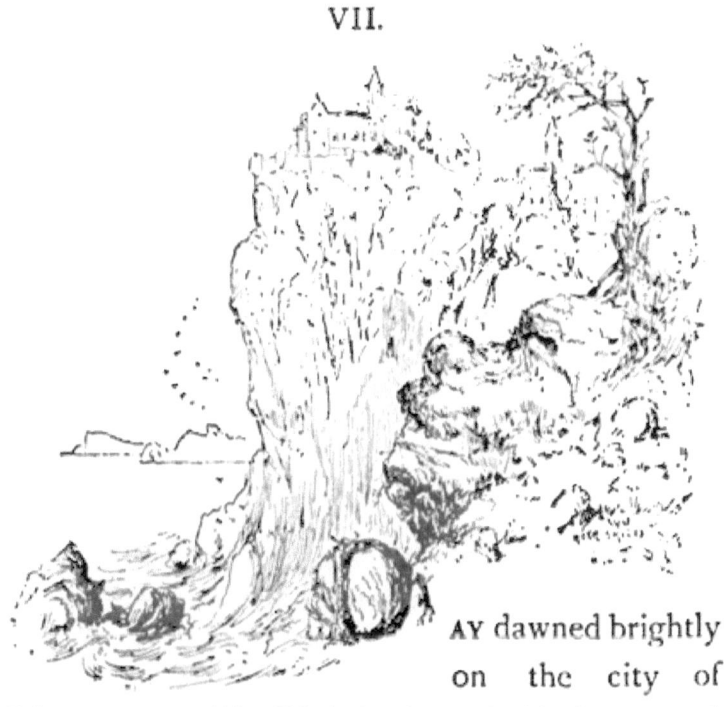

AY dawned brightly on the city of Odenvang as Yonild left the witch's barn, and with his flying shoes and invisible helmet soared above the town. It was not difficult to discern the castle-palace of the king, which crowned a rocky hill in the centre of the town, but at its southern end jutted out till it overhung the foaming sea-billows, which dashed against the precipices on which that part of the castle was built.

He descended on the courtyard ; then turning the peak of his helmet, he saw from the eyes of the sentinels that he had become visible, although still wearing the helmet of Asgard.

He went up to the nearest door, at which stood a huge giant of a man with battle-axe, horned helmet, bossed breastplate, and scaly armour, hung about with iron and brazen chains.

" I desire to speak with the princess Ionis," said Yonild.

Said the sentinel,

" There's many a gay young springald desires the same ; ay, and would give his ears to use his tongue in hers. But I trow she's entertained in better company than that of outlandish, empty-headed, feathered-heeled buffoons."

"I am no jongaleur or strolling mime," said
Yonild; "my errand is a thing of life and death;
so let me pass."

"No, by my soul," said the sentinel, "you shall
not pass. I know your kindred far too well of old.
You'd bleed the soft-hearted beauty Ionis' purse
too freely with your tale of life and death."

"I shall pass," said Yonild, endeavouring to
enter.

"Take that then for your pains," said the
sentinel, aiming a blow at the youth.

But Yonild avoided the blow, and springing
lightly into the air by the aid of his flying shoes,
spurned with his foot so deftly the huge man, that
the sentinel went rolling, roaring, and clashing
down the steps.

The rest of the soldiers came running hurriedly
to see what was to do, while Yonild entered the
palace, and turning the peak of his helmet as at
first, immediately became invisible.

On hearing the story of the sentinel, the
soldiers entered and began to search for the in-
truder, but seeing no one who answered the de-

scription they had received, they began to bully and torment their comrade for putting so silly a jest upon them.

Yonild meanwhile had entered the great hall, where the king, noble-looking, strong, and tall, sat to hear causes and see justice done to his subjects.

In a little time the queen entered. It was the lady Yonild had seen the night before at the witch's dwelling. The king made room for her on the throne beside him, but she coldly desired to be excused, and sat down with her women in an arcaded bower opening from the hall. Stealthily and eagerly the queen watched the door, looking more and more disappointed as lord and noble came in to offer his duty to the king. Suddenly her face paled, then flushed, her eyes sparkled, she shivered, and moved uneasily in her seat.

Yonild looked to see who had entered. It was a man under the middle size, but lithely made and well knit. His manner was bold and easy, and from his replies to the other courtiers, Yonild perceived his wit was quick and cutting.

When he was hailed as Garngousk by the

M

lords, Yonild knew that this was the man whose love the queen coveted, and he could not but marvel at the perversity which led her to prefer this small, dark-eyed, heavy-browed, evil-passioned, bold, forward man, to the clear-faced, tall, good, and noble-looking king.

When Garngousk had made his obeisance before the throne, he sauntered carelessly over to the bower where sat the queen and her maidens. Her eyes glistened and softened as he approached, but he scarcely looked at her as he made some politely sarcastic remarks, which almost brought tears into her eyes. Then he let his bold glances wander over the queen's maids. Some returned his glance admiringly, but many drooped beneath his gaze, while some returned him only contemptuous looks.

He did not, however, seem to see the face he sought, so he said carelessly,

" How comes it that your lady Ionis is absent from her father's hall ? "

" She went this morning to Torfrigga's house," said one of the maids.

"That is her aunt, the sister of her dead mother," said a second.

"She will return this evening," said a third.

Garngousk knit his brow closer, and an exclamation of annoyance came to his lips.

Then he went beside the queen, and threw her a careless kind word or two, at which she looked adoringly in his face.

Thinking it useless longer to delay, when he could not see the princess to warn her of her danger, Yonild left the hall, and still invisible, gained the courtyard. Springing into the air, he flew swiftly to the witch's dwelling, fearful lest he should be too late to avert the danger intended to the princess.

## VIII.

WHEN he drew near to Fanga's house, he saw the witch in the garden, gathering herbs. Turning the peak of his helmet so that he might be visible while he hovered in the air, he drew his glittering sword and gave a loud shout. The hag looked up, and fell backward in astonishment while he

swiftly descended to the earth, and stood before her with his sword pointed to her heart.

" Mercy! oh, mercy!" whined the hag.

"Wretch," said Yonild, "your evil deeds are registered, and your doom is written. You shall drink the cup you have prepared for the princess Ionis, or perish by this flaming firebrand of the gods."

"They said the gods looked on our secret sins," muttered the hag to herself, "I ne'er believed it; but now I see 'tis true. Spare me, nor cut me off in my sins; I will repent."

"Show your repentance by your acts then," said Yonild, "and you shall be spared. Exchange the potions, and let the queen drink of the venom prepared for the princess."

"I will! I will! if you will but let me live."

"Is that repentance of your crimes, to doom to horrid death the queen who fed you with rich gifts?"

"I thought you wished it, and I dread your power," said the witch.

"I tried you only," said Yonild. "This do instead. Destroy your subtle poisons that torment the flesh, and for the princess mix a harmless draught, that will induce a deathlike slumber. Mayhap the queen too will repent when she thinks her victim is within death's gates."

Then the witch replied, "Doubtless thou art

a god; thou knowest all my acts; look in my heart, and see that I resolve to obey, adore, and worship thee."

" Reserve thy worship for the Mighty One who made the heavens. I am his servant, as I hope you'll prove yourself anon."

" I swear by him who giveth victory, the father of slaughter, who nameth those that are to be slain, in all things to obey thee truly."

" Enough," said Yonild. "When the queen comes to night, give her her water of beauty if you choose, but instead of the poison she bargained for to infect and slay the princess, let her have an innocent sleeping draught that will leave no ill effects."

" I hear and will obey you," said the witch.

Yonild had turned the peak of his helmet and was again invisible. As he hovered over the witch, he said, " I will be present at your meeting with the queen to-night, although you see me not. Beware, if you deal falsely."

Then he sped back to the palace, to await the coming of the princess.

But in spite of his waiting, the princess gained the palace by a secret entrance without his knowledge.

That evening the queen received from Fanga

a harmless sleeping draught, instead of deadly poison, and innocently tinctured water, instead of the love philtre she desired. Taking her way back to the palace, she found means to administer the sleeping-draught under pretence of giving a

restorative to the princess, who was tired with her
journey.   Then hurrying to her chamber, and
throwing off her rich dress, the weak queen
pleased herself by thinking of her coming revenge.

## IX.

GREAT was the consternation in the palace next
morning when the princess was discovered lying
like one dead.

The physicians were divided in their opinions ;
some declared she was quite dead, and some
that she was only in a deep unnatural sleep.

Invisible himself, Yonild made his way into
the chamber where she lay, and stood entranced
before the sweet virginal loveliness of the princess,
which far exceeded all report.   Even while she
lay like dead, with her lovely eyes closed and her
cheek almost colourless, a deep passionate love
took possession of him, and he resolved that come
what might he would watch over her till she
awaked, so he sat invisible in a corner and heard
the talk of the king, the queen, and the physicians,

as they came and went and came again, to see if there was any change on the princess.

The sleep continuing all that day and the succeeding night, in the morning the king commanded that Ionis should be carried in a litter to the cell of a holy and skilly hermit who had his dwelling in a cave among the mountains. Though he shunned courts, palaces, and houses, the hermit never refused to use his skill for the benefit of those who came to him.

All being ready, the men took up the litter in which the princess was placed, and Yonild walked invisible beside them. After he had gone a good way, Yonild discovered that he had left his sword behind him, probably it had fallen out while he dozed during the night behind the tapestry in a corner of the princess's chamber.

Yonild blamed his carelessness, but he dared not fly back for his sword, lest he should lose sight of the princess, so he walked on, eager to catch her first glance when she awakened.

When the bearers of the litter and the princess's attendants got among the confused glens separated by wild hills which bordered the hermit's dwelling, they stopped to rest and consult about the doubtful road. While they were thus engaged, ten or a dozen men, armed and masked, came over the brow of the hill on the left hand, and with drawn swords and wild shouts rushed furiously down upon the people of the princess, who were almost quite unarmed. The attendants abandoned the litter, and fled in dismay.

Now it was that Yonild cursed his forgetfulness in leaving his sword, for he had to stand by invisible while the masked men took up the litter with the princess, and trotted rapidly across the moorland which stretched away to the right, till they came to a black chasm or pit.

Placing ropes under the litter, they proceeded to lower the princess and the litter into the pit.

Yonild wondered much at this, till one of the men who was drawing up the ropes, said,

"Well, that hard-hearted job's done; I'd as soon 'a killed a man as lowered that rope, but it's ill for a poor man to argue with a queen."

"Most like the princess is stone dead; the queen said she was, and what signifies whether she is buried in the moorland among the hills, or in a king's tomb?" said another; "yet it signifies something to us," said a third, "for we might serve many a year before we got as many gold pieces as we have got for this last two hours' work. But let us not stand prating here, but get back to the city by different ways before we are missed." Then they all set off, and soon disappeared.

Yonild flew down the pit, which widened out as he descended. When he drew back the curtains, he found that the rough manner in which she had been jolted over the ground, had awakened the Princess, and that she was sitting up and looking wildly about her.

Yonild turned the peak of his cap, and the princess saw him kneeling at her side.

"Where am I, and who are you?" said the princess.

"You are at the bottom of a pit among the hills, and I am Yonild, a friend, who would give his life to serve you."

Then he told the princess how he had discovered the queen's plot, and how he had made
the witch prepare a sleeping-draught instead of a
deadly poison, hoping that the queen would
repent of her deadly enmity when she saw the
princess lying in a death-like sleep; how the
king had sent her to the hermit, and how the
queen had interfered, and had caused her to be
put into the pit, to perish of starvation.

As Yonild knelt before Ionis, with adoration

in his eyes as he told his story, the princess regarded him with earnest looks, and becoming aware that this gallant-looking youth regarded her with more than friendly interest, she blushed entrancingly, and cast down her eyes.

Then the helplessness of their situation came into her mind, and she said,

" Is there no means of escape? must we die together in this dreadful pit?"

" There is a means of escape. You see these winged sandals which I wear; these will carry you to the upper world if you will put them on."

" Gladly would I wear them, but I cannot leave you, or accept my life at the price of yours."

" My life is at your service," said Yonild. "Fear not for that; I risk it not, for when you reach the upper air, you can untie the sandals from your feet, and wrapping them tightly together, cast them down to me. Then I shall ascend, and guide you to your father's house."

The princess agreed to this. So Yonild un- tied them, and took them off and bound them to the feet of the beautiful princess

"I am weak and dizzy," said she, "and only yet half awake. How can I fly."

"You have but to desire and try."

"I go then," said the princess, offering Yonild her hand.

He pressed it eagerly to his lips and gazed on her passionately, as, waving her hands, she soared up through the gradually narrowing pit.

She soon reached the surface of the earth, and calling down to Yonild that all was well, proceeded to untie the sandals.

But in his dread lest the sandals should come loose, Yonild had tied them so firmly that the princess could not unloose the knots.

"Cut them," cried Yonild.

"I have no knife," cried back the princess.

"Aha! I have found you," cried a voice behind her, and turning, she beheld Garngousk galloping over the soft turf towards her.

She crouched down thinking to escape ; but she was too late.

Garngousk came up, and throwing himself from his horse, tried to clasp her in his arms.

She tried to avoid him, but he seized and held her.

He reproached her for her coldness, and said that he had set out to rescue her, when the litter-bearers had returned and spread consternation through the courts of the palace by the tale of the way their mistress had been carried off.

He continued to urge her to accept him, but as she still refused, he cried,

" By fair means or foul, you shall be mine !"

Catching her up in his arms, he placed her upon his horse. Then vaulting up himself, he set spurs to his steed.

The princess cried to Yonild for help, but the horse with his double burden galloped furiously in the direction of Garngousk's castle.

## X.

YONILD, listening eagerly, heard the voice of Garngousk, and half mad with passion and fear for Ionis, tried to fly as he was wont to do, but he lacked his winged sandals, and came tumbling headlong on the earth ; then he tried to climb the

overhanging sides, but he only dislodged a mass
of stones and earth, and narrowly escaped being
crushed to death. There was neither foot-hold,
nor finger-hold. He trembled with eager passion,
and as he heard the cry of Ionis for help borne
away in the distance, he threw himself in despair
on the ground.

How long he lay he knew not, but he was
aroused by the breath of some wild animal sniffing at his face. He sprang up, and the beast
disappeared into some hole in a dark corner of
the pit.

The thought came upon him that not only was
he powerless to help Ionis, who was dearer to him
than life, but that his life would ebb away by a
miserable and lingering death. The beasts would
pick his bones, and his mother, far away in Thulê,
would never hear of him more. It was a day of
evil; first he had lost his sword, and next his
sandals; but it was the brightest day of his life,
for he had looked on, and, unblamed, had kissed
the hand of the fairest maid that the sun ever
shone upon.

The thought of Ionis roused him, and suddenly he remembered how the beast that came sniffing about him disappeared. Perhaps there was an outlet from the pit. He went to the dark corner into which the animal had vanished. The wind blew on his face, but the hole whence it came was too strait to admit his body.

Soon, however, he enlarged the opening with a pointed stone, and forcing his body in, wound himself like a worm along the narrow passage. For more than an hour thus he worked his way, sometimes half suffocated by the contractions of the tunnel; but at last it widened and increased in height, so that he was able to stand upright. Groping his way forward for a while, a turn in his path at length disclosed, far away before him, a shining point of light.

The roof was now far above his head, and the narrow passage had widened till it became a wide cavern, the sides of which eluded his touch. But he pressed onward towards the point of light which was gradually growing larger, and he gave a shout of joy when the wind brought him the

N

faint sound of the beating waves as they dashed
against the shore outside, beyond the point of
light. But even as he shouted the ground seemed
to give way beneath his feet, and he fell headlong
into a black subterranean loch. He rose quickly
to the surface, and was swimming to the farther
side, when he perceived in his fall he had lost the
invisible helmet of Asgard. He swam about,
groping for it on the surface of the water. He
dived, but dive as he might he ne'er could touch
the bottom. The point of light was hidden ; he
could only guess at the airt* it lay.

His strength was failing. He thought the
echoes roused by his splashings in the water
sounded like mocking laughter. At all hazards
he must cross this loch, whose breadth was unknown, and whose waters were benumbing and
icy cold.

He swam steadily on till his hands touched the
rocky edges of the farther side. He drew himself
wearily out of the water, and staggered on till at
last he emerged into the sunlight on the shores of
a boundless sea.

* *Airt*—Direction.

Far away to the south-west he saw the city and the palace of the king crowning the rocky headland. He was thankful for his escape with life, yet he could not forget that in a few hours he had lost all his fairy gifts. Sword, sandals of Hermod, and cap of Asgard, all were gone.

"Yet," said he, "I still have life and sunshine; if I had but food I may yet redeem my lost gifts, and with them win Ionis."

As he was speaking he descried a man laden with driftwood creeping slowly up from the rocks by the sea.

Yonild went down to meet him, and asked if he could sell or give him food.

The man put down his bundle of wood, and gazed on Yonild without speaking.

Yonild thought he had not heard, so he said, "I am faint with hunger; if you can let me have some food."

"You will be one of the gay gentles from the town o'er by," said the man, pointing away across the bays to the distant headland crowned by the king's palace.

"Nay," said Yonild, "I came from a place more distant. From Thulê I came."

"Thulê was my mother's land. You are welcome for her sake," said the man, preparing to take up his wood again.

"Stay," said Yonild; "I am younger than you, and can carry this more easily."

"E'en as you will," said the man, moving slowly away.

Yonild took up the wood and followed, till the man came to his dwelling, which was half hut half cave.

Food being set before him, Yonild, as he ate, asked the man if he knew where Garngousk dwelt.

"I do truly. I know his castle as a place to shun."

"He has carried off the princess by force," said Yonild.

"She is not the first by many."

"But this is Ionis, the daughter of the king."

"Kings make themselves whiles by force, whiles by fraud; his daughter is but a woman after all," said the man · then he added, "but this

is a good king—so the folk say, at least—so I'm
sorry for his loss."

When his meal was ended the man directed
Yonild how he should find Garngousk's castle,
although he advised him to give up his purpose,

and avoid the place, for it was guarded by fierce
dogs, and fiercer men.

" I will go," said Yonild, though the place was
full of raging fiends."

" Well, well," said the man, " if you will go, go
as a jongaleur ; you can play and sing, doubtless.
Here is my gittern, it is old and battered, but
many a one would give much to have it for an
hour, for no one can refuse what the player wills."

Yonild eyed it curiously, and passed his fingers
over the strings ; it seemed as if he had awakened
a being who lived in the instrument, the music
was so weird, so piercing, and expressive, and so
unlike the sound of any other gittern.

Yonild thanked him cordially, and set off on
his journey.

Yonild reached the castle of Garngousk without trouble. When the fierce dogs came bounding
out to devour him, he swept his hand over the
gittern strings while walking boldly on, and the
snarling dogs, with lowered tails, went skulking
back to their kennels. At the sound of the music
the men came out, and as he played, Garngousk

sent a page to bid Yonild come into the hall to amuse his fair guest.

Ionis started when she saw him, but quickly concealed her agitation.

Garngousk scowled on Yonild, and said, " Sing us a song of love which overcame all obstacles.

Yonild chanted in rhythm the story of a knight who gained his lady in spite of the enchantment by which she was holden.

It was a rough and unpolished song, but the entrancing music of the gittern made it sound of more than earthly grandeur.

Every one was charmed. Garngousk tossed a purse to Yonild, who did not stoop to pick it up. The princess rose and presented him with something she took out of her long hanging sleeves.

It was the sandals of Hermod.

Everybody laughed to see this man, who did not think it worth while to pick up a purse, receive so thankfully a pair of old shoes.

Yonild bound them firmly on his feet. Then rising said, " I can dance as well as sing." Pacing the hall lightly and airily, he danced to the music

of the gittern such steps as never before were seen.
When he reached the hall door he cried to Garngousk, "Be on your terrace in one hour from this
time, and I will show you greater wonders." Then
he gave a look of assurance and hope to the princess, and swiftly withdrew.

He flew back rapidly, by the help of the flying
sandals, to the hut of the man, and returned him
his magic gittern, and procured from him a lighted
torch ; with this he flew into the dark cavern, and
found the helmet of Asgard between the rocks
where he had fallen into the water.

Putting the helmet on his head, he flew swiftly
to the king's palace, and passing invisibly into the
princess's chamber, he found his sword behind the
tapestry where he had lain the night before.

## XI.

YONILD came flying back wearing the helmet of
Asgard. When he came in sight of Garngousk's
castle, the sun had set, though his light could still
be seen in the northern sky. As he drew nearer.

he perceived two figures on the terrace that jutted out from the castle and overhung the sea. His heart bounded when he saw it was Ionis and Garngousk. The princess was endeavouring to elude Garngousk's embrace, and when at last he caught her in his arms, she gave a wild shriek for help.

Yonild gave a loud shout, and turning the peak of his cap, became visible, as he flew swiftly through the air towards the pair on the terrace.

Ionis gave a cry of joy when he descended beside her. Garngousk, although he had started back at the appearance of the winged stranger, soon recovered himself, when he perceived in Yonild the jongaleur who had been playing in the castle that day.

"Juggler or god, angel or fiend," he cried, "you shall not come between me and my purpose; begone, and leave us."

Ionis clung to Yonild, who said, "Willingly I leave you, but this fair lady goes with me to her father's house."

"Take then the punishment which is the due

of meddling knaves," said Garngousk, drawing his sword, and darting at Yonild's heart.

Yonild stepped aside, and drew his flaming blade from its sheath.

" Let us go in peace, or your blood be upon your own head," said he, standing upon his guard. For he had never yet killed a man, and was loth to slay Garngousk if he could gain his purpose without his death.

" My voice speaks in my sword," said Garngousk, as he again tried to plunge his blade into Yonild's heart.

Yonild parried the blow, and struck back at Garngousk, who laughed as he evaded the stroke, for he saw that Yonild was not equal to himself in fencing skill. But what Yonild wanted in skill, he made up for in coolness, so the two slashed at each other without either receiving more than a few flesh wounds.

In the midst of the fight it came into Yonild's mind that he was not availing himself of his sword's rarest quality. So, instead of aiming at Garngousk, he smote at his sword with his own bright glancing weapon. Garngousk's sword was cut through clean near the hilt, and his life seemed at Yonild's mercy. "Now yield thee, and beg forgiveness of this lady for the wrong you have done her, and of the greater wrong which you intended her, and your life shall yet be spared."

"I ask my life from neither man nor maid. Look to your own life," said Garngousk, springing so suddenly at Yonild's throat, that he had to drop his sword in order to grapple with his adversary.

They swayed and tugged as they grappled, getting nearer and nearer to the edge of the terrace which overhung the sea, as they struggled. Now they were at the edge, and Garngousk lay half over the low parapet which was the only guard, but still he clung fiercely with one arm round Yonild's neck, while with the other he showered blows upon his body. When he found himself losing his footing, he clung to Yonild with both hands, as if resolved that he would not go alone over the precipice.

"Once more," said Yonild, "do you yield?"

"Never!" gasped Garngousk, tugging fiercely at Yonild, as if careless of saving himself, but only wishful to carry his enemy with him.

Yonild dis-

engaged his right hand, and smote Garngousk a crashing blow on the breast, his arms relaxed ; then, before Garngousk could recover himself, Yonild gave him another terrible blow under the chin, at same time bowing his head to let the arms of Garngousk slip over him.

Garngousk lost his hold; his feet stepped and slipped wildly on the outside of the parapet; then he fell head foremost over the precipice, and was dashed to pieces on the rocks that jutted out of the sea.

Garngousk's men had been astonished at the noise, but as they had been forbidden by their master to approach the place, whatever sounds they might hear, they knew not what to think, when Ionis, led by Yonild, again invisible, entered the hall and commanded horses. The servants, struck with fear at hearing a man's voice in the middle of the hall, where no man was to be seen, got the horses ready with all speed, and Ionis went off, seemingly accompanied by a horse with an empty saddle. This was the steed on which Yonild sat. An hour's riding brought them to the palace of the king, who, unable to sleep, was pacing eagerly backwards and forwards in the hall.

Ionis and Yonild were joyfully received, and the women rushed to tell the queen that Garn-

gousk was slain, and the princess rescued by the
gallantest knight that ever was seen.

All her plots frustrated, the lover for whom
she had so sinfully and cruelly schemed lying
dead, despair seized on the weak and hapless
queen. That night she threw herself headlong
over the palace rocks into the sea. Her dead
rock-battered body was found by some fishermen,
who carried it up the steep pathway to the palace.

The same night the dwelling of Fanga, the
witch, was seen wrapped in flames. No one
could tell whether she had perished or escaped,
but she never appeared in Atlantis again.

The king employed Yonild in all his most
difficult and delicate services ; in the field against
his enemies, and in the court in forming treaties
with his friends. Yonild's intrepidity and justice,
united to the influence of the magical gifts of
Fail-me-never, the sandals of Hermod, and the
helmet of Asgard, everywhere crowned with success whatever he undertook, and the kingdom of
Atlantis grew in purity, richness, and strength,
day by day.

After a time Yonild yearned to return to his friends in Thulê. Neither Ionis nor Yonild knew how dear they had become to each other till the day of parting drew near. Then the love which had been so long untold took words to itself, and filled the pair with inexpressible delight.

The king consented to their marriage, which took place with such splendour, such gifts to the poor, and such entertainments to the whole people, that the sages said that they had reached the highest point of the golden days of Atlantis.

During the honeymoon Yonild freighted a ship with rich presents for his old friends in Thulê, and with his bride set sail to revisit his birth-land.

That sea which he had passed over in darkness, and almost despairingly, when the sandals of Hermod bore him from Thulê, now glittered in sunlight.

Yonild sang to the sound of harp as Ionis stood playfully against the mast, keeping time with uplifted hand and gracefully swaying figure to the sounds of the music.

When they reached Vasader in Thulê, they found his mother happy and young-looking. Thiblun, her husband, had been kind and affectionate, ever since the day of Yonild's disappearance. Whether this was due to his remorse for his treatment of the lad, or to the spells which Thrudur, the good witch, wove that night around the castle walls, none can tell.

Yonild offered back the magic gifts to Thrudur, fearful lest at any time they might fall into unworthy hands, but Thrudur bade him keep them without such fear, assuring him that the Nornir would take care that their gifts were not vainly nor wrongly bestowed.

After spending fair and happy days in Thulê, Yonild and his bride set sail, and arrived safely in Atlantis.

When the old king died, Yonild ascended the throne, and ruled with such wisdom, justice, and kindness, that the people never

ceased to bless the time that he came over the
sea, borne up by the wondrous sandals of
Hermod.

HERE was a young, rich, and beautiful lady, who was about to be married to a lord. A day or two before the wedding, the lord brought his friend, a gallant and handsome young farmer, to see the lady of his choice. The lady fell in love at first sight with the farmer, and ere they parted, the farmer was as deep in love with her.

When the morning of the wedding had come, the lady, love-sick for the young farmer, instead of betaking herself to the kirk to be married, took to her bed, and the wedding was put back. Nevertheless, in the afternoon, she disguised her face, and dressing herself in manly apparel, went with crossbow on her shoulder, and with her dogs at her heels, to hunt on the grounds of the young farmer, which was part of her own estate.

She crossed and recrossed the fields, whistled and hallooed to her dogs, without meeting the farmer. As she was beginning to fear that he was absent, and was about to withdraw, she met him coming up the road.

She professed to be surprised to see him, as she understood he was to be at the wedding to give away the bride to the lord.

"Ah!" said the young farmer with a sigh, "I would she were as poor as myself, that I might ask her to give herself to me."

"Are you then in love with the promised bride of the young lord your friend ? How would you answer to him, should the lady favour your hopes ?" said she.

"With sword and axe I would give him a meeting, and let the best man win."

At parting, the lady drew from her pocket a glove embroidered with gold, and said to the farmer,

"Here is a glove I picked up on the way thither; as I am a stranger here, I will leave it with you in order that you may find the owner."

Next day she sent out the crier to say that she had lost a glove embroidered with gold, and that she would take the man who found it for her husband, if the man was willing.

The young farmer heard the proclamation, and, half wild with joy, and half doubting his good fortune, took his way to the house of the lady. He presented the glove, and modestly reminded her of the reward promised to the finder, and although that reward was far above his hopes, it was what his heart most ardently desired.

Before he left her, she confirmed the promise of the crier, and agreed to take him for her husband. The report was soon spread abroad, and coming to the young lord's ears, he demanded that the farmer should resign his claim to the lady, or else meet him in single combat.

The farmer answered that he would never resign the lady while there was breath in his body, but that he would meet the young lord when and where he pleased, and with whatever weapons he liked to choose.

Swords and bucklers being chosen, on the day appointed for the fight, the lord and the farmer, accompanied by their seconds, or shield-bearers, and their friends, met to settle their difference. With the assistance of their shield-holders the combatants warded off each other's blows for some time; but at last the farmer clove his adversary's shield in twain, and following up his advantage, brought the young lord to his knees by a blow on his helmet.

Then putting his sword to his throat, he made

the young lord resign all claim to the lady, and beg his own life.

Soon the handsome young farmer and the rich and beautiful lady were married, and after a time she told him of her device of the glove, and how the game that she hunted that day with her dogs and her crossbow was the young farmer himself. Both agreed that for the hunter and the hunted that hunting was the happiest that had ever been undertaken in Thulê.

www.ingramcontent.com/pod-product-compliance
Lightning Source LLC
Chambersburg PA
CBHW020626030726
47497CB00007B/2433